'I can't believ[...]
It's been tw[...]
divorce, Liam, [...]
that time did you make any
attempt to talk to me. So why
have you suddenly decided that
it's time we sort things out?'

'Because it might be two years but I haven't
come to terms with what happened even if
you have! What happened between us left
scars, Sophie. The only way we can rid
ourselves of them is by talking it all through
and getting the truth out into the open at last.'

'You want the truth, do you? Well, the truth is
that I don't give a damn about what happened
in the past. It's over and done with, and all
I'm interested in now is the future...'

Jennifer Taylor lives in the north-west of England with her husband Bill. She had been writing Mills & Boon® romances for some years, but when she discovered Medical Romances™, she was so captivated by the heart-warming stories that she set out to write them herself! When she is not writing or doing research for her latest book, Jennifer's hobbies include reading, travel, walking her dog and retail therapy (shopping!). Jennifer claims all that bending and stretching to reach the shelves is the best exercise possible.

Recent titles by the same author:

SAVING DR COOPER
HOME BY CHRISTMAS
HIS BROTHER'S SON
LIFE SUPPORT

A VERY SPECIAL MARRIAGE

BY
JENNIFER TAYLOR

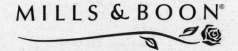

First published in Great Britain 2003
Harlequin Mills & Boon Limited,
Eton House, 18-24 Paradise Road, Richmond, Surrey TW9 1SR

© Jennifer Taylor 2003

ISBN 0 263 83466 2

Set in Times Roman 10½ on 12 pt.
03-0903-52734

Printed and bound in Spain
by Litografia Rosés, S.A., Barcelona

CHAPTER ONE

HAD she made a terrible mistake?

As she stepped out of the taxi into the bustle of Palma harbour, Sophie Patterson suddenly found herself beset by doubts. Up till that point she'd been quite confident that she was doing the right thing. She'd handed in her notice at work, given up the lease on her flat and said goodbye to her friends, sure in her own mind that she'd made the right decision, yet all of a sudden she found herself wavering.

Had she been right to turn her back on everything she knew? Maybe it *did* feel as though she'd been in a rut ever since her divorce but how could she be sure her life would improve by making such drastic changes to it?

Sophie grimaced because it really wasn't the right time to start having second thoughts. The letter she'd received had made it clear that she should report for duty at eleven a.m. sharp and it was almost that now. Picking up her suitcase, she scanned the dock.

Several of the major holiday companies used the harbour at Mallorca to berth their vessels and it was difficult to decide which of the liners moored there was the one she would be working on for the next three months.

Mindful of the minutes ticking away, Sophie hurried along the quay, sighing in relief when she discovered that the ship nearest to her was the *Esmeralda*. There was a member of the crew on duty at the bottom of the gangplank, checking names against a list, so she waited in line until it was her turn.

'I'm Sophie Patterson. The new nurse.'

'Welcome to the *Esmeralda*, Miss Patterson.' The young man put a tick against her name. 'If you'd like to board the ship, the purser will direct you to your quarters.'

'Thank you.'

Sophie squared her shoulders then made her way up the gangplank. There were a lot of people milling about when she reached the deck, mostly people like her, she guessed, hired to look after the passengers, so once again she waited in line until it was her turn to speak to the purser.

'I'm Sophie Patterson, the new—'

'Nurse.' The good-looking, fair-haired young man smiled at her. 'Welcome aboard the *Esmeralda*, Miss Patterson. I am Yuri Markov, the chief purser. My role is to make life as easy and uncomplicated as possible for staff and the passengers alike. So if you have any problems whilst you are on board ship, please, do not hesitate to consult me.'

'Thank you.' Sophie returned his smile, feeling a little colour touch her cheeks when she saw the admiration in his eyes. She had steadfastly avoided any involvement with the opposite sex in the two years since her divorce and it was rather flattering to realise that she could have this effect on an eligible male. 'That's very kind of you.'

'It is easy to be kind to a beautiful young woman like yourself, Miss Patterson.' Yuri's smile was warmer than ever and Sophie laughed, her deep blue eyes sparkling with amusement.

'Now you're flattering me!'

'I was merely stating the truth.' Yuri's gaze held hers fast for a moment before he glanced at the list he held. 'Your cabin is in the hospital bay, Miss Patterson. I shall get a steward to show you the way.'

'Please, call me Sophie,' she said quickly, her head

whirling because she wasn't used to being showered with compliments like this. It seemed ages since anyone had made such a fuss of her, not since the early days of her marriage, in fact, when Liam had never let a day pass without making sure she'd known how much he'd loved her.

The memory still had the power to hurt so Sophie hastily put it from her mind as Yuri summoned a steward and told him to take her to the hospital bay.

He turned to her as the man picked up her case.

'Perhaps you would do me the honour of joining me for dinner tonight, Sophie? I shall add your name to my table if you don't think I am being too presumptuous?'

'Thank you. I would like that very much,' she declared, throwing caution to the winds. She managed to hold her smile when Yuri took her hand and raised it to his lips, but she couldn't ignore the soulful way he was looking at her.

'This promises to be a wonderful trip,' he murmured.

Sophie quickly withdrew her hand and hurried after the steward, relieved to make her escape before the situation developed. It did make her see how long it had been since she'd played the dating game, however. She'd met Liam when she'd been just nineteen and they had married a year later. She'd had little experience of men before her marriage and none since. One of the first changes she would have to make would be to bring her ideas in line with more modern thinking. The days of one man, one woman and happy ever after had long since gone out of fashion!

'This is the hospital bay, Miss Patterson. I may as well give you a tour while we're here.'

The steward, whose name badge identified him as Charlie Henshaw, elbowed his way through the swing doors. He nodded towards a door on their right. 'Through there is the clinic where you and the doc will see your patients each morning and over there is the operating theatre.'

'I didn't realise there was a theatre on board!' Sophie exclaimed, peering through the glass pane set in the door. She took rapid stock of the state-of-the-art facilities and sighed. 'It's far better equipped than some of the NHS hospitals where I've worked.'

'The ship's owners had the hospital bay refurbished last winter and decided to install a theatre while they were at it,' Charlie explained. 'Doc Hampson wasn't keen on the idea but they thought it would be a big selling point. A lot of passengers feel happier knowing there are proper medical facilities on board if the worst happens. It's certainly increased trade because we're fully booked all season.'

'I see. Why wasn't Dr Hampson keen on the idea, though?' Sophie asked curiously, following the steward along the corridor. She glanced into a small sick-bay furnished with all the usual equipment she would have expected to see in any modern hospital ward. The difference was that the room was beautifully decorated in a soothing sea green and there were tasteful water-colours on the walls.

'The doc's a nice old chap but he just isn't up to operating nowadays.' Charlie stopped as they came to the end of the passage. 'It's high time he retired, in my opinion. He might have reached that conclusion himself because I just heard that he's not joining us this trip. They've had to hire a last-minute replacement for him.'

'Oh, dear! I had no idea,' Sophie exclaimed. The elderly doctor had sat in on her interview and had seemed very pleasant. It was rather daunting to discover that she would be working with a complete stranger for the next few months.

'This is your cabin, miss. It's not exactly luxurious—none of the crew's quarters are—but there's everything here that you'll need. The doc's cabin is just across the passage.'

Sophie tried to shrug off her concerns as she looked around the cabin. It was very compact but, as Charlie had said, there was everything there that she would need during her stay. A single bunk bed and combined vanity and wardrobe unit would solve her sleeping and storage problems whilst the tiny *ensuite* bathroom with its shower cubicle, basin and lavatory would fulfil her other needs.

'It's fine,' she said, turning to smile at the middle-aged steward. 'I've lived in nurses' quarters in the past so I'm used to not having a lot of room to spread myself around.'

'You'll only really need it for sleeping,' Charlie advised her, lifting her case onto the bed. 'You and the doc are regarded as officers whilst you're on board so you'll have free run of the ship. You'll be able to use the lounges and other facilities—that's if you can cope with folk coming up to you all the time and asking about their ailments!'

'I shall bear that in mind!' She quickly hunted in her bag for some change as the steward turned to leave, but he stopped her with a shake of his head.

'No need for that, miss. We're all here to work so none of us expect tips. If you need anything, just use the bell and give me a buzz. The passengers won't arrive until late afternoon so we're not too busy at the moment, although it will be bedlam later.'

'Thanks, Charlie.'

Sophie decided to unpack after the steward left then explore the ship and get her bearings. She unlocked her case, then hung her clothes in the wardrobe, smiling to herself when she saw how colourful they looked.

Buying herself some new clothes had been another step on the way to remodelling her life and an enjoyable one, too. She'd gone a bit mad, in fact, choosing the bright cotton outfits which she planned to wear in her off-duty time. While she was working she would wear a smart new uniform but the colourful clothes had been chosen in a fit of defiance. The old Sophie Patterson no longer existed and in her place was a woman who intended to make the most of her life instead of wasting it.

All of a sudden Sophie felt her doubts disappear beneath a renewed surge of excitement. She had been right to do this. Three months spent cruising the Mediterranean and then the world would be her oyster!

Dinner on the first night, she'd been told, was always an informal affair and casual clothes were the order of the day. She showered and changed into white cotton jeans and a vivid blue T-shirt then ran her fingers through her short blonde hair until she'd achieved the spiky look which the hairdresser had told her suited her so much. She'd had her hair cut only the previous week and she still wasn't used to the new style, although it was certainly easier than the shoulder-length bob she'd had before. A quick wash and her hair was done!

Stepping in front of the mirror, she studied herself critically. She had to admit that the end result was rather pleasing. The vivid blue of the T-shirt was the perfect foil for her colouring although she experienced a momentary qualm when she read the logo that was printed in sequins across its front.

Telling herself that it was just a bit of fun, she let her gaze move on and nodded in satisfaction when she saw what a difference the new make-up she'd purchased had made. Her eyes looked enormous thanks to the mascara and shadow whilst the lipgloss made her mouth look seductively full. The only flaw she could spot was the tiny mole at the corner of her mouth but there was nothing she could do about that. Anyway, Liam had always said that it made him want to kiss her...

Sophie blanked out that thought. She'd promised herself that she wouldn't look back but focus on the future and at the present moment that meant dinner. She left her cabin then paused when she saw that the door to the cabin opposite hers was open. She hadn't heard the doctor arriving but she could have been in the shower at the time. It was a shame that she'd missed him because she would have liked to have broken the ice by introducing herself.

She glanced at her watch but there were still ten minutes to spare before she needed to be in the dining room. She tapped on the door and grimaced when she heard a muffled voice calling from the bathroom to come in. She hadn't realised he was getting ready for dinner but she could hardly walk away now that she'd knocked on the door.

She looked curiously around as she went inside but the cabin was an exact replica of her own, apart from the fact that it was nowhere near as tidy. It looked as though the doctor must have unpacked in rather a hurry because there was a heap of clothes tossed onto the bed and a stack of books piled haphazardly on the bedside cabinet.

She wandered over to look at them, grinning when she saw the eclectic mix of paperback thrillers and weighty medical tomes. Obviously, her new colleague believed in being prepared for every eventuality.

'Sorry to keep you waiting.'

Sophie felt the shock hit her like an actual physical

blow when she heard the man's voice. She rocked back on her heels and had to grab hold of the cabinet to steady herself. She knew she should turn round but it was impossible to move a single muscle. It couldn't be him! a small voice was screaming inside her head. It was just her mind playing tricks…

'Are you all right, Sophie?'

There could be no mistaking who he was now that he'd called her by name, even though he'd spoken to her in a tone she hadn't heard him use for a long time. Their last conversations had been so angry and bitter that it still made her feel sick whenever she thought about them. It felt as though a lifetime had passed since she'd heard such concern in his voice.

'For pity's sake, say something, Sophie. Don't just stand there looking as though your worst nightmare has come true!'

There was a catch in that deep voice now, an echo of pain that made her ache as well. She was actually trying to think of a way to comfort him when it struck her what she was doing.

This man had broken her heart and he most certainly didn't deserve her pity!

Anger gave her the strength to turn and face her ex-husband at last. 'What are you doing here, Liam? Exactly what is going on?'

Liam could feel the waves of antipathy flowing across the cabin and suddenly found it impossible to think clearly. Why hadn't he allowed for the fact that he would feel so…*emotional*? he wondered dazedly.

'I'm the new ship's doctor,' he said tersely, struggling to keep a grip on himself. He'd known when he'd accepted the post that Sophie might be upset by the thought of them working together, but he'd told himself that he would find a way to convince her it would be all right. All he wanted was a chance to set matters straight and it had seemed like the perfect opportunity to do so. The last few months had convinced him that he needed to lay the past to rest, once and for all.

'Th-the new doctor?'

Liam's hands clenched when he heard the tremor in her voice. It was obvious how shocked she was and he suddenly found himself wondering if he was being selfish. Maybe Sophie had come to terms with the past and he was in danger of opening up wounds that had already healed? Just because he hadn't been able to rid himself of the memories, it didn't mean she'd had the same problem. He only had to look at her to see how much she had changed, in fact.

His slate-grey eyes skimmed over her as he drank in the differences two years had brought about. The new hairstyle suited her, he realised in surprise, even though he would *never* have expected her to opt for such a funky style. Sophie's choice of hairstyle and clothing had been very conservative in the past but there was nothing conservative about that spiky halo of blonde wisps or about the outfit she was wearing, for that matter.

Liam's mouth curved into a reluctant smile when he read the logo on the front of her T-shirt. *Treat me like a princess!* it implored, and it amused him greatly although he couldn't for the life of him imagine the old Sophie wearing anything like it. Ditto the snug-fitting jeans which hugged her pert little bottom like loving hands.

His smile faded abruptly as his gaze travelled on. Although she was of no more than average height, she had incredibly long legs and the tight jeans set them off to perfection, highlighting their shapeliness. Liam felt a funny buzzing sensation in the pit of his stomach and hastily lowered his eyes another few inches. He just managed to bite back his gasp when he saw her bare toes peeping through the straps of her sandals.

She'd painted her toenails bright *blue* to match her T-shirt but Sophie had *never* worn nail polish in the past. Even if she had, she certainly wouldn't have dreamt of wearing such a crazy colour. Adding up everything he'd seen—the funky hairstyle, the trendy clothes, the nail polish—and he was more convinced than ever that he'd made a massive error of judgement. Sophie had moved on with her life and the proof of that was clear from her appearance. How could it be fair to rake up the past when it would be bound to upset her?

'Let's get this straight, Liam. Are you saying that you're going to be working on board this ship?'

Liam took a deep breath when he heard the mounting anger in her voice. Maybe he had made a mistake but there was little he could do about it now except to try and make the coming weeks as easy as possible for both of them.

'That's right. I've signed on for the summer season,' he explained, trying to disguise his hurt when he saw her mouth thin with displeasure. Surely he hadn't been foolish enough to hope that she might be pleased to see him?

'Dr Hampson has decided to retire,' he continued hurriedly before the idea could take root. He knew why he'd taken the job and it had nothing whatsoever to do with winning Sophie over. 'Apparently, he's been having chest pains and his consultant has advised him to take things easy. I was hired at the last minute as his replacement.'

'So you had no idea I would be working on this ship when you took the job?'

Liam saw her frown as she tested out that theory and

sighed. He was tempted to take the easy way out but he wouldn't be able to live with himself if he didn't tell her the truth. There'd been enough half-truths in the past and he refused to let them spill over into the present.

'No. One of your friends at the Royal Memorial told me that you'd got a job on board this ship when I went up there to see you. She wasn't sure when the *Esmeralda* actually set sail but she gave me the name of the agency who'd hired you so I could check with them.' He shrugged. 'To cut a long story short, I phoned them and during the course of the conversation they mentioned they were looking for someone to replace Dr Hampson so I offered my services.'

'This just doesn't make sense!'

She shook her head so that the spiky wisps of blonde hair shimmered as they caught the glow from the overhead light. Liam's hands clenched again but this time because he had an almost irresistible urge to run his fingers through that silky halo. All of a sudden he could remember with alarming clarity just how soft her hair had always felt, how wonderful it had smelled when he'd woken each morning and taken her in his arms...

'You seem to have gone to a lot of trouble to track me down, Liam, but surely it must have occurred to you that you were the last person I would want to work with? I would have thought I'd be the last person on your list, too, so what is going on? Why did you really take this job? If it was your idea of a...a *joke* then I have to say that I don't find it the least bit funny!'

Liam dragged his mind back from such nonsensical thoughts when he heard the fury in her voice. 'I didn't do it as a joke, Sophie. Far from it. I realised a couple of months ago that we needed to talk to one another. There are a lot of things we need to sort out so when I found out there was a job going on board the *Esmeralda*, it seemed like too good an opportunity to miss.'

'I can't believe I'm hearing this!' She put her hands on her hips and glared at him. 'It's two years since our divorce, Liam, and not once in all that time did you make any attempt to talk to me. You didn't make much of an effort before that either, so why have you suddenly decided that it's time we sorted things out?'

'Because it might be two years but I haven't come to terms with what happened even if you have!'

All of a sudden Liam could feel his own anger igniting. He took a couple of steps, which were all it needed to cross the cabin. He stared down into her angry blue eyes, feeling the pain welling inside him as the memory of all the hurtful things they'd said to one another came rushing back.

Sophie should have trusted him! She should have had enough faith in him to know that he would never have had an affair!

'What happened between us left scars, Sophie, and I'm not too proud to admit that either. The only way we can rid ourselves of them is by talking it all through and getting the truth out into the open at last.'

'You want the truth, do you?' She laughed shrilly. 'Well, the truth is that I don't give a damn about what happened in the past. It's over and done with, and all I'm interested in now is the future.'

'So you've put it all behind you, have you? Every single thing that happened no longer means anything to you?'

He couldn't keep the bite out of his voice and he saw her flinch. When she went to push past him he caught hold of her arm and made her stop.

'Maybe you've erased me from your memory, Sophie, but can you honestly say that you've forgotten our child?'

His fingers tightened as grief suddenly overwhelmed him. 'Look me in the eyes and tell me that you've forgotten about Zoë and then I'll believe you when you say that we have nothing to talk about!'

CHAPTER TWO

'DAMN you, Liam! Damn you to hell for doing this!'

Sophie's voice broke on a sob and Liam felt his anger drain away when he saw tears streaming down her face. He already had hold of her so it was the easiest thing in the world to pull her into his arms and cradle her against him.

She felt so small and fragile that he was terrified of hurting her if he held her too tightly, yet he needed to hold onto something as all the pent-up emotion suddenly spilled from him. Two years ago he'd been too numb with grief to cry but now he couldn't hold back his tears as the memories came flooding back.

Sophie had been six months pregnant when a routine check-up had shown problems with their baby's development. The placenta had become detached from the wall of the uterus, depriving the unborn child of vital nutrients and oxygen. A decision had been taken to deliver the baby and Sophie had been rushed to Theatre for an emergency Caesarean section.

It had been a little girl and Liam could still recall how perfect she had been when the doctor had placed her in his arms for a few, precious seconds before she'd been taken to the intensive care unit. They had called her Zoë and she had lived for just one week before her tiny body had given up the struggle for survival.

Sophie had been inconsolable afterwards and he simply hadn't known how to comfort her. It had broken his heart to see how devastated she'd been so that he'd found himself staying later and later at work to avoid going home. And then one fateful night, a few months after Zoë had died, his own grief had caught up with him.

He'd gone out after work and, for the first time in his life, he'd got so drunk that he hadn't known what he'd been doing. If it hadn't been for one of the nurses taking him back to her flat, he would have spent the night on the streets. He'd been so ashamed afterwards that he'd let Sophie think that he'd spent the night at work but, some-how, the story had got out about him spending the night at Amanda's flat and Sophie had accused him of having an affair…

'Let me go.'

Liam jumped when he heard the steely note in her voice. He quickly released her and ran his hands over his face to wipe away his tears. Sophie had her back to him but he could tell that she was struggling to regain her composure. He touched her lightly on the shoulder, want-ing to comfort her in some way, but she shrugged off his hand.

'Don't!'

Liam dug his hands into the pockets of his towelling robe. It hurt to know how much she hated having him touch her, but what had he expected? The days when she would have melted into his arms were long gone and too much had happened since to recapture the magic they'd once known.

'Are you all right?' he asked gruffly, trying not to dwell on how painful he found that thought. He wanted to lay the past to rest, not rekindle the embers of a dead love affair, he reminded himself sternly. It was the reason why he'd been so anxious to see Sophie again. It had become increasingly clear in the past few months that he would never be able to get on with his life until they had sorted out the mistakes they'd made, although the likelihood of them sorting *anything* out seemed non-existent at the moment.

'I'm fine. Don't worry about me. There's no need.'

She headed for the door but Liam knew that he couldn't just let her walk away without trying to smooth things over. Maybe his plan hadn't gone as he'd hoped it would but they were going to have to work together in the coming weeks so they at least needed to behave in a civilised manner with one another.

'Look, Sophie, I apologise. Maybe this was a lousy idea but all I can say in my own defence is that I never meant to upset you.' He shrugged when she glanced back. 'I know it won't be easy but we're going to have to find a way to resolve our differences so we can work together.'

'You really think I'm going to work with you?' She laughed and Liam felt his insides twist when he heard the scorn in her voice. 'I'm sorry to disappoint you, Liam, but it isn't going to happen. I have absolutely no intention of working with you, now or in the future. Now, if you'll excuse me, I'd like to go and pack.'

'There's no point because you aren't going anywhere.'

He knew that he should be trying to appease her rather than confront her, but her unyielding attitude stung. Maybe Sophie had moved on but her feelings towards him certainly hadn't improved.

'I shall do whatever I want!' She glared at him, her eyes filled with contempt. 'The days when you had any say over what I do, Liam Kennedy, are long gone!'

'I have no intention of trying to stop you leaving, Sophie, but I'm sure the captain will.'

He went to the porthole and pulled back the curtain, feeling a wave of weariness wash over him. Sophie wasn't interested in talking about the past and he really couldn't blame her. He should have tried harder at the time to convince her that nothing had happened when he'd stayed at Amanda's flat. But he'd been so hurt that Sophie had believed he would betray her and she'd been too angry to listen to him. Neither of them had been thinking clearly because they'd been so devastated by the loss of their precious child. It was that thought which made him soften his tone.

'It may have escaped your notice but we've already set sail. We're currently heading out into the middle of the Mediterranean and, from what I can remember of our itinerary, we won't reach land until tomorrow morning. Even then, do you really think it would be fair to just up and leave?'

He sighed as he let the curtain fall back into place. 'There's several hundred people on board this ship and any one of them could need our help at a moment's notice. Surely it would be better if you contacted the employment agency in the morning and asked them to find a replacement for you? It would mean us making the best of things for a few days, but I promise you that I'll do my bit if you'll meet me halfway. So what do you say, Sophie?'

'I...I don't know.'

She bit her lip and Liam could tell how difficult she was finding it to make up her mind. He crossed the cabin but this time he didn't make the mistake of touching her. Sophie had made it clear how she felt about that.

'We've worked together in the past, and successfully, too, so surely we can manage to do so again for a short time,' he said softly, refusing to dwell on how distressing he found the idea. 'I'd offer to leave but the people at the agency made it clear that they'd had problems finding a suitably qualified doctor. I wouldn't want to leave the passengers in the lurch.'

'No, it wouldn't be right,' she agreed reluctantly.

She took a deep breath that made her small breasts rise beneath the close-fitting T-shirt and Liam just managed to stifle his groan when he felt his body respond with a fervour that shocked him. He drew the robe around him, relieved that its bulk concealed his predicament. He'd not exactly led the life of a monk since their divorce but he couldn't recall responding so wholeheartedly to any woman in the past two years, not even Julia.

The thought threw him into confusion so that he missed what Sophie had said. 'I'm sorry, what was that?'

'I just said that we shouldn't need to see each other all that much.' She shrugged but this time Liam wisely kept his eyes on her face and didn't let them stray. 'Once we've seen any patients who turn up for morning surgery then that should be it, basically.'

'Of course,' he agreed, trying to appear positive, no easy task in view of the way his mind was churning. He'd honestly and truly believed that he was ready to get on with his life and that all he needed to do was to draw a line under the past. But how could he be ready to plan his future when he was still so *susceptible* to his ex-wife's charms?

'And so long as the agency can find a replacement for me then there shouldn't be a problem?'

'It might take them a few weeks to find someone suitable,' he warned, deciding it would be better to focus on this problem rather than start digging up any others. 'Experienced nurses of your calibre don't exactly grow on trees.'

A touch of colour ran up her face but she didn't acknowledge the compliment. 'I'm sure they'll find someone eventually.'

'And what about you, Sophie? What will you do?' He

frowned as he thought about the implications of her having to leave the ship. 'Maybe you could return to the Royal Memorial? I'm sure they'd be delighted to take you back.'

'They probably would but I've no intention of going back there. The reason I left in the first place was because I needed a change of scene. Don't worry about me, Liam, I'll find something else, maybe go abroad. There's a lot of nursing posts advertised in the USA so that's one option.'

'So what you're saying is that you're completely flexible?' Liam couldn't keep the surprise out of his voice.

'Yes. The world's a big place and I've seen far too little of it.'

'And there's nothing to tie you down to any one place?' he insisted, because he couldn't help being surprised by her attitude. The Sophie he remembered had been a homebody, not an adventurer. It made him see just how great the change in her had really been.

'Nothing and nobody,' she stated firmly. 'So if you're trying to find a diplomatic way to ask if I'm involved in a relationship then don't bother. I think the phrase which best sums up my feelings is once bitten, twice shy.'

'It wasn't all bad,' he protested, because it was painful to realise how much their divorce had affected her. Sophie had always had a very loving nature and he hated to think that she'd ruled out the possibility of finding happiness again even though the thought of her finding it with another man didn't sit comfortably with him, strangely enough.

'You're entitled to your view,' she said dismissively. 'Anyway, what about you, Liam? Is there someone special in your life?'

Liam pushed the troubling thought aside because he

needed to deal with the question. For some reason it seemed incredibly difficult to decide how to answer it. It wasn't that he was afraid of upsetting her—Sophie had made it perfectly clear that he no longer featured in her life—but he felt rather *awkward* about discussing his plans with his ex-wife. Crazy though it undoubtedly was, it felt as though he was letting Sophie down.

The idea was just so ludicrous that it immediately cleared his mind of any doubts. 'Actually, there is. Her name is Julia and she's a doctor, too. We met while we were both working overseas, although she's from London originally.'

He shrugged because there was no point holding back the most important bit now he'd got this far. 'We're thinking about getting married later this year, in fact.'

'I see. So it appears that congratulations are in order.'

Liam frowned when he heard what sounded suspiciously like a catch in her voice. He breathed a sigh of relief when she treated him to a brilliant smile because he wouldn't like to think that Sophie had been upset by his announcement.

'I hope you and the second Mrs Kennedy will be very happy, Liam. I certainly hope the marriage works out better than ours did!'

'Ah, so there you are, Sophie! I was just coming to find you. I thought you had got lost.'

'I'm afraid I got delayed. Sorry.'

Sophie summoned a smile as Yuri greeted her at the entrance to the dining-room. She followed him across the room, murmuring her thanks when he pulled out a chair for her to sit down. Glancing around, she repeated her apologies for the benefit of the other diners seated at their table.

'I'm sorry I'm late.'

'Don't you worry your pretty little head about it, young lady.' The elderly American gentleman on her left smiled at her. 'If my wife wasn't sitting right here beside me, I'd tell you it was well worth the wait!'

The blue-rinsed matron next to him raised her eyes. 'Take no notice of Randolph, honey. He's all talk these days! Anyhow, you've only missed the introductions and that isn't a problem. I'm Gloria Walters and this is my husband, Randolph. We're from Georgia and this is our first trip to Europe. We're trying to see as much as we can, which is why this cruise is such a great idea.'

'I'm Sophie Patterson, the ship's nurse,' Sophie explained. She jumped when someone approached her, but it was only the waiter wanting to drape a napkin over her knees. She smiled her thanks but she could feel her heart beating in time to the sentence that was reverberating inside her head: *Liam is getting married, Liam is getting married.*

'Oh, we already know that. Yuri here told us all about you,' Gloria assured her.

Sophie had no idea what the purser had said but it was a relief not to have to go into detail about her role on the ship. She smiled and nodded as the rest of her table companions introduced themselves, though she doubted if she would remember many of their names later.

Discovering she would be working with Liam had been a big enough shock but learning that he was getting married had been much worse, and yet she couldn't understand why she felt so devastated. Their marriage was over and she most certainly didn't want to resurrect it, but she couldn't help feeling bereft at the thought of Liam marrying another woman.

'And here is our final guest. Excellent! We shall be able to enjoy the evening now.'

Yuri placed his hand lightly on her shoulder as he stood up, and Sophie flinched. She felt as nervous as a kitten, her whole body vibrating with a fine tremor that was making her feel sick.

She picked up her water glass and took a sip of the cool liquid in the hope that it would steady her, but all it took was the sight of the purser greeting Liam to make the tremor increase. It appeared that Liam would be joining them for dinner and the prospect of having to make conversation with him was more than she could bear. It was only the thought of the scene it would cause if she got up and left that kept her sitting there.

'Allow me to introduce our new doctor.' Yuri swiftly made the introductions, smiling charmingly when he came to Sophie. 'I'm not sure if you two have met yet.'

'Dr Kennedy and I have already introduced ourselves,' Sophie said hurriedly.

'Indeed we have,' Liam agreed smoothly, but she could see the question in his eyes. She knew he was wondering how much she intended to tell everyone, but if he thought she was about to admit that they'd once been married then he could think again.

'Yes, we bumped into each other earlier.' She turned to Yuri as Liam took his seat and smiled warmly at him. 'Tell us about your job, Yuri. It must be fascinating, meeting so many new people all the time.'

The purser needed little encouragement and happily began regaling them with tales about the trials and tribulations of being a purser on a busy cruise liner. He was an amusing raconteur and the rest of the group were soon showering him with questions.

Sophie was very aware that Liam was making no at-

tempt to join in, however. She shot him a wary look and
flushed when she discovered he was watching her. There
was something in his eyes, a hint of some emotion she
couldn't quite decipher...

'And what about you, Sophie? You must tell us all
about your job now.'

She jumped when Yuri placed his hand on hers. She
was aware of the knowing looks that were being exchanged around the table and quickly tried to move her
hand out of the way, but he held onto it.

'It must be fascinating, being a nurse. To hold the
power of life and death in such delicate hands.'

He sighed expressively and Sophie coloured. There
must be little doubt in the minds of anyone watching that
the purser was interested in her and it made her feel uncomfortable, especially with Liam there to witness what
was happening.

'I hate to disillusion you but a nurse's role is rather
more mundane than that.'

She eased her hand out of his grasp and picked up her
glass. 'My job is to carry out orders and care for a patient's needs. It's the doctors who have the real power.'

'Is that a fact? So how does it feel, Dr Kennedy, to
know the buck stops with you?' Randolph leant across the
table and smiled at Liam. 'It must put a lot of pressure
on you, young man.'

'It can do but you learn to adapt to the stresses of the
job. I certainly don't spend too much time dwelling on
the thought that I hold the power of life and death in my
hands,' Liam explained dryly. 'Anyway, helping a patient
recover is a team effort. It needs both doctors and nurses
to achieve results.'

'Spoken like a true diplomat!' Gloria declared. She

turned to Sophie and winked. 'Looks as though you two should get along just fine, honey.'

Sophie smiled, although she was sorely tempted to tell the older woman that she wouldn't be around long enough to find out. First thing tomorrow morning she would contact the agency and ask them to find a replacement for her. Fortunately, the waiter arrived just then with their first course and the conversation moved on to other topics. Even so, it was a relief when dinner was finally over and she could make her escape.

Yuri looked disappointed when she announced that she was having an early night. 'Are you sure I can't change your mind, Sophie? There's dancing on the promenade deck tonight and I would be honoured if you would agree to be my partner.'

'That's really kind of you, Yuri, but it's been a busy day and I'm exhausted.'

She moved aside so that Liam could pass them, feeling a frisson run through her when his arm brushed hers. In accordance with the dress code for the evening, he was wearing a casual, short-sleeved shirt and she could feel the silky, dark hairs on his forearm tickling her bare skin as he moved past.

One of the other guests stopped him and Sophie felt another ripple run through her when she heard him laugh at something the woman said. Liam had always had the most wonderfully infectious laugh, so deep and warm that it had made everyone around him want to laugh, too. How strange that she'd forgotten all about that until now but, then, they'd had very little to laugh about in the months leading up to their divorce.

The thought was so painful that she knew she had to get away. When Yuri tried again to persuade her to stay she shook her head. 'I'm sorry but I really am very tired. I'll see you in the morning, I expect.'

She hurriedly left the dining-room and made her way to her cabin. The passengers were making the most of the first night of their holiday and she didn't meet anyone on the way. She undressed and slid on a pair of the new shortie pyjamas which she'd bought for the trip. The bunk bed felt rather cramped after the comfort of a double divan, but she was both physically and mentally exhausted. She was fast asleep when someone banged on her cabin door an hour later.

Sophie scrambled out of bed and ran to answer the summons, peering blearily at Liam. 'What's the matter?'

'There's been a fight between two of the crew. One of the men has been stabbed and he's in a pretty bad way, apparently. The other guy's also been hurt, although he's not as bad.'

His gaze skimmed over her before he abruptly swung round. 'Put some clothes on. I'll meet you in the clinic in five minutes.'

Sophie took a deep breath as she closed the door. She felt completely disorientated, having been woken up like that. She went into the bathroom and splashed cold water on her face then quickly hunted some clothes out of the wardrobe and dressed. There wasn't time to brush her hair but she doubted if it would matter. Liam probably wouldn't notice how she looked.

Her mind hiccuped to a halt because all of a sudden she could picture the expression in his eyes all too clearly. There had been something so spine-tinglingly familiar about the way he'd looked at her just now that a rush of heat suffused her.

Sophie bit her lip but she could feel the excitement building inside her and it scared her. She didn't want to feel this awareness around Liam but she couldn't seem to stop what was happening any more than he'd been able to do. The thought brought her up short.

If Liam was planning on getting married again, why had he looked at her—his ex-wife—with such hunger?

CHAPTER THREE

WHAT the hell had he been thinking?

Liam cursed roundly as he tossed a handful of sterile dressings into his bag. He must have been stark, raving mad to stand there staring at Sophie like that! So maybe it *had* only been for a split second but she must have noticed. What woman wouldn't notice when a man was ogling her?

Another oath leapt from his mouth as he added a giving-set and several pairs of disposable gloves to the collection. It was rare that he ever swore but he was allowed a lapse at a time like this. He'd stood outside Sophie's door positively *drooling* over the sight of her in those sexy little pyjamas. It didn't make him feel good to admit what he'd done, yet he knew that he would do exactly the same thing again in similar circumstances. The sight of her shapely body in that strappy little top and shorts get-up was enough to make any red-blooded male stare!

Liam groaned as an image of Sophie suddenly swam before his eyes. Her blonde hair had been all tousled and her face had been softly flushed with sleep. One strap of the pyjama top had slipped down her arm so that the cotton fabric had dipped at the front, affording him a tantalising glimpse of her small breasts. The shorts had definitely lived up to their name, leaving her legs completely bare from the tops of her slender thighs right the way down to her shapely ankles, and he ground his teeth when he felt his body react predictably to the memory. He had to get a grip. Lusting after his ex-wife really wasn't an option!

'What can I do to help?'

Liam swung round when he heard Sophie's voice coming from the doorway and let out a sigh of relief when he saw the jogging pants and over-sized T-shirt she was wearing. At least his self-control wouldn't be put to the test again that night, it seemed.

'We'll need saline for starters. Can you see if you can find some? Oh, and check the drugs cupboard and see what we've got in the way of pain relief. Here's the keys.'

'Thanks.'

She caught the bunch of keys he tossed to her and hurried to the cupboard. Liam left her to go through it as he double-checked that he had everything they might need. He didn't want to have to start running backwards and forwards for all the things he'd forgotten.

'It's really well stocked. I found some morphine so shall I sign for it or would you prefer to do it?'

Liam shook his head. 'I don't have a problem with you signing it out. So long as it's accounted for then it doesn't matter which one of us completes the paperwork.'

'Fine.' She quickly filled out the necessary form then relocked the cupboard door. She handed him the keys, along with two ampoules of morphine, then took a couple of syringes out of a box on the shelf and gave them to him as well.

Liam nodded his thanks as he stowed them in his case. 'Don't forget the saline.'

'I won't.' She quickly found the bags of saline and passed them to him. 'Is that everything now?'

'Hopefully.' He snapped the locks on the case and stood up. 'I'm not sure exactly what we're going to find.

All I know is that one man has been stabbed and that the other isn't as badly injured.'

'We could be dealing with anything, then,' she observed as she followed him from the clinic. 'I wonder what the fight was about?'

'I didn't ask. I was more concerned about what we would have to deal with.' He smiled wryly as he locked the clinic door. 'I was looking forward to a complete change of scene when I took this job, too. I had visions of treating patients with nothing more serious than seasickness. I should have known better!'

Sophie laughed. 'You should! It was tempting fate to hope for an easy ride, although I certainly didn't expect anything like this to happen.' She looked at him curiously. 'What did you mean about a complete change of scene, though?'

Liam sighed as he elbowed his way through the swing doors. 'I was working for a foreign aid agency in Africa until last month. The area I was working in is on the edge of a war zone so stabbings and shootings are pretty much an everyday occurrence there. It was a real culture shock at first, although I soon got used to it.'

'Why on earth did you take a job like that?' she exclaimed.

'Because I wanted to make a real difference to people's lives.' He led the way to the stairs, wondering if that had sounded as ridiculously idealistic to her as it had to him, even though it was the truth.

'And did you? Make a difference to people's lives, I mean?' she asked quietly.

'I like to think I did, but who can say for sure? The people I dealt with are so poor that death is an everyday occurrence. If they don't get shot or stabbed then more often than not they die from malnutrition.'

'It must have been difficult, working in conditions like those. I had no idea...'

She stopped and Liam saw a shadow cross her face. His heart ached because he knew immediately what had caused it. Once upon a time they'd been so close that each had known what the other had been thinking, and it hurt to realise how far apart they'd grown.

'There's no reason why you should have known where I was working, Sophie,' he said gently.

'No, I don't suppose there was.' She summoned a smile. 'I must confess that I'm rather surprised, though, because you never mentioned that you were interested in doing aid work.'

'It was only after we split up that I decided to find a new direction for my life,' he explained. 'It helped to put my own problems into perspective when I saw the difficulties other people have to contend with on a daily basis.'

'And does Julia work for the aid agency as well? You said that you'd met her when you were both working overseas.'

'She's done aid work ever since she qualified,' he explained flatly, wondering why he felt so uncomfortable talking about Julia. He forced a little more enthusiasm into his voice.

'She's a superb doctor and completely devoted to her work. It's thanks to her that the agency has managed to establish a base in the region, in fact.'

'I see. So does that mean you'll be returning there to work after you're married?'

Liam shrugged, not wanting to admit that he and Julia hadn't reached a decision about where they would live. Julia was keen to continue her work but he wasn't sure if it was what he wanted to do on a long-term basis. One of the reasons why he'd returned to England when his contract with the aid agency had ended had been because he'd hoped it would help him make up his mind. He needed to be sure before he committed himself to working overseas permanently, although how Julia would react if he decided against it was another matter.

'I'm not sure yet,' he said, hurriedly dismissing the thought because it was pointless worrying when there might be no need. It could turn out that his inability to make a decision was all tied in with the fact that he needed to resolve things with Sophie. In which case, all his problems would be resolved at once.

'We're still very much at the planning stage—' he began, then broke off when one of the ship's officers came hurrying to meet them as they reached the lower deck.

'Dr Kennedy?'

'Yes. I'm Liam Kennedy and this is Sophie Patterson, the ship's nurse.'

'I'm glad to meet you, Dr Kennedy. You, too, Miss Patterson.'

The man shook hands then quickly led them along a corridor. 'I'm Mike Soames, the chief petty officer. I'm still trying to establish exactly what happened but, basically, two of the crew started fighting and one guy pulled out a knife and stabbed the other fellow.'

'Whereabouts did the knife penetrate?' Liam asked, wanting some idea of what they could be dealing with.

'In the chest,' Mike informed him. He opened a door and stepped back. 'Alexei—that's the chap who's been stabbed—is in here, but I thought it would be best to separate them so I've put Grigorio in the next cabin. The men who would normally use these cabins are bunking down in the crew's lounge for the night.'

'Good. I was hoping we wouldn't have an audience,' Liam said gratefully, turning to Sophie. 'Will you check out the chap next door while I see to this fellow? If you're happy that he's not too badly injured then you can come back and help me.'

'Of course.'

'I'll go with you, Miss Patterson,' Mike Soames said hurriedly.

Liam went into the cabin as the chief petty officer accompanied Sophie next door. The patient was lying on one of the lower bunks and Charlie Henshaw—the steward who'd shown Liam to his cabin when he'd arrived—was with him. He looked relieved when Liam appeared.

'I'm glad you're here, Doc. I've done a bit of first aid in my time but this is way out of my league.'

'Let's take a look, then.'

Liam crouched down beside the bunk. He could tell immediately that the man was in a very bad way. His pupils were fixed and dilated and his breathing was extremely laboured.

He quickly removed the blood-soaked towel from the man's chest and whistled when he saw the knife wound. Although it was fairly small, it was obviously deep. 'That doesn't look so good. How many times was he stabbed, d'you know?'

'Just the once. One of the other guys managed to break up the fight.' Charlie shook his head. 'It all happened in a flash. One minute they were arguing and the next second Grigorio had pulled out a knife and stabbed Alexei.'

'Well, it's certainly gone in deep. There could be all sorts of damage to the major organs.' Liam glanced round when the door opened and Sophie appeared. 'How's the other fellow doing?'

'A few bruises and a bump on the back of his head but he'll live.' She glanced at the man on the bunk and pulled a face. 'He doesn't look too good, though.'

'He doesn't. Can you check his blood pressure while I get a line into him? He desperately needs fluids. It also looks as though he's going to need to be intubated so I'll give him an anaesthetic to relax his muscles once everything is set up,' Liam explained, quickly tapping up a vein and inserting a line into the back of the man's hand.

Charlie took the bag of saline from him once he'd set up the drip, and hung it on the end of the top bunk. Liam nodded.

'Thanks. I need to establish an airway now but I could do with a bit more light so I can see what I'm doing.'

'Leave it to me, Doc.'

Charlie hurried away and returned a few minutes later with one of the huge torches that were normally used for signalling to other ships. Liam smiled his approval as the steward angled the beam so that he could set to work.

'That's great. I can see where I'm aiming for now.'

He administered the anaesthetic then quickly inserted an endotracheal tube and established an airway. Once it was secured, he immediately started the patient on oxygen.

'Blood pressure is dropping,' Sophie warned. 'Pulse is very weak, too.'

'Could be a haemothorax,' Liam said, taking a scalpel out of his bag. 'The knife appears to have entered the chest at an angle so it's possible the left lung has been damaged. I'll see if I can relieve the pressure.'

He made a small incision under the man's left armpit then used a pair of forceps to open the muscles between the ribs, but there was no sign of blood in the pleural cavity. 'That's not it. How's he doing now?'

'BP is still going down rapidly.'

Sophie suddenly leant forward and checked the pulse at the base of the man's neck. Liam held his breath be-

'cause he had a horrible feeling that she wasn't going to find one.

'No pulse. He's arrested!'

'It looks as though his heart must have been damaged, then,' Liam exclaimed. 'If enough blood has collected in the pericardium, it will have stopped his heart beating. We need to get him on the floor so we can start CPR.'

Sophie grabbed the man's legs while Charlie gave him a hand to lift the seaman off the bunk. Liam turned to Sophie. 'I'll need you to give me a hand opening him up.'

'You mean you're going to do a thoracotomy?' she exclaimed incredulously. 'Here?'

'I don't have a choice. External cardiac massage won't work if the pericardium is full of blood so I'm going to have to open his chest to do it. We don't have the time to get him up to Theatre because his brain will stop functioning in three minutes without any oxygen reaching it.'

He didn't waste any more time on explanations. Slipping the scalpel into the hole he'd made already under the man's armpit, he sliced horizontally across the patient's chest. Sophie was searching through his bag—finding scissors and dressings—and he breathed a sigh of relief. It was reassuring to know that he had someone with her experience to help him and didn't have to explain every little detail to her. It left him free to get on with his job.

'Oh, my Gawd!' Charlie muttered as Liam took the pair of scissors from her and began to cut through the tough layer of muscle beneath the patient's skin.

'I know it looks brutal but it's his only chance.' He reached the breastbone and felt beads of sweat gather on his forehead as he struggled to saw through the bone. Every second that passed meant that the chances of the patient surviving were decreasing. He grunted in relief when he felt the last bit of the bone give way so that he was able to complete the incision.

'What I wouldn't give for some retractors,' he muttered, struggling to see inside the chest cavity.

'What's them, Doc?' Charlie asked curiously.

'Great big metal clamps that you use to open up the chest,' he explained. 'Where's that torch? Thanks.'

He peered into the chest cavity while Charlie held the torch for him, and immediately spotted the cause of the problem. As he'd suspected, the pericardium—the sac surrounding the heart—was bulging with blood and preventing the heart from beating.

'Definite signs of tamponade.' He grasped the sac with a pair of narrow forceps and managed to cut through it. However, when it came to removing the blood clot, it proved impossible. His fingers were just too large to fit through the limited amount of space he'd been able to make.

He turned to Sophie. 'See if you can get those clots out of there, will you? Your hands are smaller than mine.'

She quickly changed places with him and he saw the tip of her tongue poke between her teeth as she inserted her fingers through the opening in the chest wall. Liam felt a wave of heat rush through him and looked away because it shocked him that he should be so responsive to her at a time like this.

Why hadn't he allowed for this when he'd taken the job? he wondered incredulously. He'd been attracted to Sophie from the first moment they'd met, when she'd been a student nurse and he'd been a brand new houseman, yet it had never crossed his mind that he might still feel the same about her. Why should it have done when he was committed to Julia?

His heart began to thud because that question had naturally led to a second, one it was even more difficult to answer.

If it was Julia he loved then why did he feel this desire for Sophie?

Sophie held her breath as she inched her fingers through the narrow gap. If anyone had told her she'd be helping to perform major surgery on the floor of a cabin, then she would have laughed out loud. But if Liam thought they could save the man's life, she would give it her best shot.

Relief swept through her as she finally managed to reach the blood clot. She scooped it out of the way and dropped the bloody mass on the floor beside the bunk.

'Got it!' she declared triumphantly, glancing up. She frowned when she saw how abstracted Liam looked. He looked as though he was miles away, a worrying thought in view of the seriousness of what was happening.

'Liam?' she prompted anxiously, and saw him jump.

'You've got it out? Good work!' He made an obvious effort to collect himself. 'Now, see if you can encourage the heart to start beating again. There's not enough room to massage it so try flicking it with the tip of your finger.'

Sophie followed his instructions and felt her excitement mount when the man's heart suddenly fluttered. She tried it again and laughed when she felt it start to beat. 'It's working!'

'Right, we need to get him up to Theatre, stat.' Liam was all business once more as he got up. 'We need something to use as a stretcher. Can you sort it out, Charlie?'

'No problem, Doc.'

The steward hurried away as Sophie sank back on her heels. 'Do you think he'll make it?'

'With a bit of luck, but we're going to have to stop that bleeding.' He frowned in concern as he watched a few drops of blood ooze out of the man's chest. 'That wound needs stitching as soon as possible—can you get every-thing ready in Theatre? I don't want to have to waste precious time setting up once we get him there. It's going to be touch and go as it is.'

'Of course.' She scrambled to her feet and stripped off her blood-soaked gloves and dropped them on the floor then grimaced when she saw the mess they'd made. 'This place is going to need a thorough cleaning before the crew can use it again.'

They both looked round when the door opened and Charlie appeared with Mike Soames in tow. Sophie saw Mike turn a delicate shade of green when he saw all the blood, and sympathised with him. The cabin must look like a scene from a horror film to the uninitiated.

'Did you find us something to use as a stretcher?' Liam demanded, oblivious to the petty officer's distress.

'I've commandeered one of the kitchen trolleys,' Charlie explained. 'It's too big to get it in here so we're going to have to carry Alexei outside.'

'That shouldn't be a problem with the three of us,' Liam declared.

Sophie hoped he was right and that poor Mike wouldn't pass out before they managed to get the injured seaman onto the trolley. It was amazing how many grown men she'd seen keel over at the sight of blood.

There was no time to worry about it, however, because she had more important things to do. She ran back upstairs to the hospital bay and quickly scrubbed up then slid on a gown and a fresh pair of gloves. She'd been a theatre nurse for a number of years and it was reassuring to slip back into the familiar routine. She laid out the instrument trolley then unpacked sterile drapes to cover the patient during the operation. By that time Liam had arrived.

'I need to scrub up,' he told her tersely, shooting an anxious look at the man lying on the stainless-steel kitchen trolley. 'We're going to have to be quick, though, because he's losing a lot of blood.'

'I'll take him through while you get ready,' Sophie assured him. 'Who's going to do the anaesthetic, though?'

'Me.' Liam's tone was grim. 'It's times like this when you could do with an extra pair of hands, isn't it?'

'We'll manage.' She smiled at him and saw his grey eyes darken before he abruptly turned away.

'I'll be as quick as I can,' he said gruffly.

Sophie wheeled the patient into Theatre, trying to decide exactly what she'd glimpsed in Liam's eyes just now. She sighed when it struck her how pointless it was to worry about it. Once her replacement arrived she would be leaving the ship and she doubted if she and Liam would ever meet again. The thought gave her very little pleasure, oddly enough.

Liam must have got ready in record time because barely a minute had elapsed before he elbowed the door open. He had Charlie Henshaw with him and Sophie raised her brows when she saw that the steward was gowned and gloved as well.

'Charlie has offered to help,' Liam explained, going straight to the trolley. He nodded to Charlie. 'Let's get him on the table.'

Sophie didn't question his decision as she hurriedly draped the patient. If Liam thought that Charlie would be of use then that was fine by her. He was preparing the anaesthetic now—checking the settings on the machines then attaching the tubes which would provide sufficient drugs to keep the patient unconscious during the operation. It was obvious that he knew what he was doing, too.

'Looks as though you've done that a time or two,' she

observed lightly, swabbing the man's chest. Blood was oozing out each time his heart beat so she checked the bag of fluid to see if it needed replacing.

'More times than I care to count. I had to be anaesthetist, surgeon, physician and general dogsbody in my last job. There certainly wasn't any point standing on your professional dignity when there was just Julia and me to deal with every patient who turned up at the clinic.'

'It must have been tough,' Sophie said quietly, because hearing him speak about the difficulties he and Julia had encountered made her heart ache. Once upon a time *she* would have been the one to share such experiences with him.

She shrugged off the thought as Liam instructed Charlie to keep an eye on the monitor that registered the patient's blood pressure and heart rate, and to tell him immediately if there was any change. She and Liam had had their chance at happiness and it hadn't worked. What had she told him earlier, that it was a case of once bitten and twice shy? Well, that applied doubly in this instance. She would never make the mistake of falling for her ex-husband again!

The operation progressed remarkably smoothly, given all the problems they faced. Sophie had to admit that she was impressed by Liam's expertise. He handled the delicate operation of stitching up the hole in the patient's right ventricle with a skill and panache that she'd rarely witnessed during her time in Theatre. By the time it came round to closing the patient's chest, she was confident about the outcome.

'You did a great job,' she said sincerely as Liam administered the drugs which would reverse the anaesthetic. The patient was now ensconced on a proper hospital trolley and would shortly be moved to the sick-bay.

'Thanks, but I couldn't have managed without your help, or Charlie's for that matter.' Liam smiled as he stripped off his mask. 'You two make a great team!'

'All part of the service, Doc,' Charlie observed cheerfully then chuckled. 'Wait till I tell my missus that I assisted at an operation. She's mad keen on all those hospital dramas on the telly and she'll be really impressed!'

'And so she should be.' Liam clapped the steward on the shoulder. 'Remind me to buy you a drink as a thank you.'

'I'll hold you to that, Doc.' Charlie suddenly grimaced. 'And now I'd better get that trolley back to the kitchen. The chef is going to be less than impressed when he finds out what it's been used for.'

'If you have any problems, just give me a call and I'll sort it out,' Liam told him. He turned to Sophie after the steward left. 'Rather a baptism of fire, wouldn't you say?'

'I would. A bit more exciting than handing out tablets for sea-sickness.'

'Just a bit!' Liam chuckled, a throaty sound which made the tiny hairs on her arms stand to attention. 'I'd forgotten about your dry sense of humour, Sophie. You always did make me laugh.'

'Not always,' she said, bending to pick up the bag of rubbish because she didn't want him to see how much that comment had stung. In the weeks leading up to their divorce they'd had very little to laugh about and the memory still had the power to hurt.

'No. We had bad times, too, didn't we? Far too many of them at the end. But it wasn't like that in the beginning, was it? We seemed to spend most of our time when we were together having fun.'

'Did we? I really don't remember.'

She quickly sealed the sack and elbowed her way out

of the door. She wasn't sure what the procedure was for disposing of surgical waste so she turned round to ask Liam and felt her heart ache when she saw the sadness on his face. Was he thinking about how much joy they'd found in one another's company? She might have claimed not to remember how wonderful it had been, but it had been a lie.

She was filled with a sudden and overwhelming sense of loss. Liam had been her whole world at one time and she'd been his. How had they allowed themselves to lose all that they'd had?

CHAPTER FOUR

LIAM took a deep breath but the pain in his heart wouldn't budge. His mind seemed to be awash with memories of all the wonderful times he and Sophie had enjoyed together. He had honestly believed that he'd found his soul mate when he'd met her, and that they would be together for ever, but it had all gone so terribly wrong.

Why hadn't he tried harder to make her understand that nothing had happened between him and Amanda that night? he wondered sickly. If he hadn't allowed his pride to get in the way, they might never have got divorced. Granted, they would still have had to work through their grief over Zoë's death, but it had been Sophie's belief that he'd had an affair which had brought things to a head. He'd made a terrible mistake by not making her listen to him, but maybe it wasn't too late to rectify matters.

He'd actually opened his mouth when it struck him what he was doing. He was trying to patch things up with Sophie *not* because he wanted to draw a line under the past but because he hoped they could recapture the magic they'd once known. Fine, but where did that leave him and Julia?

Liam's head swam so that it was a second before he realised that Sophie had spoken to him. 'I'm sorry. What did you say?' he said huskily, praying that she couldn't tell how shocked he felt. Julia was a wonderful woman and he both admired and respected her. It made him feel like the lowest form of pond life to even consider letting her down.

46

'I asked what I should do with this waste.'

'Just leave it there for now. I'll check with Mike Soames and find out what the procedure is for disposing of it.'

Liam saw her frown when she heard the tremor in his voice, and hastily cleared his throat. It had been a temporary lapse, he assured himself, a small blip on the route to everlasting happiness which he would achieve once he and Julia were married. It was natural that he should feel rather…*nostalgic* about the past, but it certainly didn't mean that he didn't love Julia. How could he not love a woman who was as self-sacrificing and dedicated—not to mention beautiful—as Julia was?

He took swift advantage of the return of common sense. 'Everything else can be left for the cleaners. Once we've moved the patient into the ward, that's basically it for tonight.'

'Surely he's going to need monitoring?'

'Of course, but it won't need both of us to do it. You get yourself off to bed once we've got him settled. I'll sit with him.'

'You can't stay with him for the whole night,' she protested. 'What's going to happen tomorrow when we hold our first surgery? You'll be worn out.'

'I doubt we'll have many people turning up so early in the trip,' he replied dismissively. 'Anyway, I'm used to functioning on very little sleep so it isn't a problem.'

'We could take it in turns. If you do the first shift, I can take over from you in a couple of hours' time.'

Liam shook his head, although he knew it would make more sense if they shared the task. It was just that he preferred to do it himself rather than sit there, wondering how long it would be before Sophie appeared to relieve him. Maybe she'd be wearing those sexy little pyjamas that she'd had on earlier…

He shut off that thought before it could get him into any more trouble. He'd allowed his libido quite enough leeway for one night. 'There's no need for that. I can manage. Now, if you'd just help me get him to the ward, we can both get some rest.'

He saw her mouth draw down at the corners when she heard the authoritative note in his voice but he refused to feel bad about pulling rank. It was for her good as well as his, even though she obviously didn't believe that.

They took the patient to the ward and made him comfortable. Sophie didn't wait for Liam's instructions as she did the man's obs and noted them on a chart which she hung on the end of the bed.

'His BP, pulse and respiration are all within acceptable limits,' she informed him in her most professional manner. 'Temperature is normal.'

'Good.' Liam played his part, refusing to let her see that it stung to have her treat him as a work colleague. He could hardly complain when he'd been the one to instigate this. 'That's it, then. You may as well get off to bed now.'

'Fine. Goodnight.'

She didn't say anything more before she left the room. Liam sighed as he drew up a chair. Sophie wouldn't readily forgive him for playing the heavy-handed boss but there was little he could do about it now. At least he had the comfort of knowing that one of them would get a good night's sleep, which was something.

He decided to write up the patient's case notes while he had the chance. Once they reached port the following morning, the injured seaman would need to be transferred to hospital and he wanted to be sure the doctors there had a full account of everything he'd done.

It took some time to write it all down and he yawned as he put the cap back on his pen. It was two a.m. and time he got some rest. He checked the patient's obs once more then settled down in the chair. Normally he had no problem sleeping but the moment his eyes shut he started getting flashbacks to what had gone on that night.

He made himself breathe slowly and deeply but it was hopeless. Images flashed through his mind like stills from a film: the shock on Sophie's face when she'd discovered they would be working together; the way that damned purser had leered at her over dinner—here Liam ground his teeth; the way her face had lit up when their patient's heart had started beating…

He sighed as he opened his eyes and got up. Sitting there, mulling over everything that had happened, was only making matters worse. Maybe it would help to settle him down if he read for a while?

He went to his cabin to find a book and spent several minutes trying to decide if he should gen up on possible problems arising from major thoracic surgery or simply relax with the latest paperback thriller he'd bought at the airport. He grimaced as he finally opted for the textbook. His conscience would give him gyp if anything happened and he hadn't prepared for it.

Taking the book off the pile, he turned to leave then stopped when a piece of paper fell out of the pages of the book and landed on the floor by his feet. He picked it up, frowning when he saw that it was a photograph of Julia. She had given it to him the night before he'd left for England but he'd forgotten that he'd put it in the book so it wouldn't get creased.

Now he studied the photograph while he thought about

the woman he was going to marry. Julia was a wonderful person and he admired everything she stood for. She was also extremely beautiful with those classical features and that mane of chestnut hair. He knew how lucky he was to have found someone like her, yet as he stood there he was once again beset by doubts.

Could he really imagine spending the rest of his life with Julia? Was it what he truly wanted?

Liam sighed because far too many times in the past few weeks he'd asked himself those very same questions, and he couldn't understand why he had such difficulty making up his mind. Everything pointed to the fact that he was making the right decision yet there was something holding him back.

Even Julia had sensed his uncertainty because she'd told him that he needed to be sure it was what he wanted before they got married. As Julia had pointed out in her usual pragmatic fashion, she didn't want him looking back in a couple of years' time and wishing that he'd not gone through with it.

It had been partly to allay her concerns as well as his own that he'd decided to return to England, in fact. He'd sensed that his doubts stemmed from the fact that there were so many loose ends that needed tying up. He and Sophie had parted on such bad terms and he was honest enough to admit that it still troubled him. To his mind, it had made sense to see her again and resolve their differences because once he'd done that he would be free to find the happiness he craved with Julia. However, as he stood there, studying the photograph, Liam felt an ache suddenly settle in his heart.

As beautiful and as talented as Julia was, she still wasn't Sophie. Could he ever really love her as much?

* * *

Sophie spent a restless night. So much had happened that her mind kept churning it all over. She tossed and turned until in the end she simply admitted defeat and got up. It was just gone five and the sun was rising, turning the sea blood-red as it skimmed the horizon.

She slipped on shorts and a T-shirt, pushed her feet into a pair of trainers then left her cabin. A brisk walk around the deck should clear her head and prepare her for the day ahead. She had to pass the ward on her way out but she didn't stop. Liam had made it plain that he didn't need her help and she had no intention of interfering.

Surprisingly, there were a number of people about when she reached the promenade deck. A few were jogging but the majority were simply enjoying the sunrise. Sophie spotted Randolph Walters sitting on a deckchair near the rail and stopped to speak to him.

'I see you're an early bird, too, Mr Walters.'

'I like to be up with the sun,' Randolph told her. 'At my age it seems a shame to waste your time lying in bed when you can be up, enjoying yourself. You never know how long you have left!'

'I'm sure you have many years ahead of you,' Sophie declared with a smile. 'In fact, if you'd like my professional opinion then I'd have to say you look extremely fit.'

'I'd say the same about you, my dear, only I'm not sure if it's permissible for a gentleman to say such things to a young lady nowadays.' Randolph winked at her. 'I'd hate to tread on any politically correct toes, you understand.'

'You aren't treading on any toes so thank you for the compliment, although I have to confess I don't feel very fit after the night I've just had.'

'That sounds intriguing,' Randolph observed curiously. 'Dare I ask what you were up to?'

'Oh, we had a medical emergency so it was rather late by the time I got to bed.'

Sophie hurriedly skated over the facts because it wouldn't be right to go into detail. Quite apart from the matter of patient confidentiality, she doubted if the captain would want it broadcast that members of his crew had been involved in a brawl.

'And on your first day, too,' Randolph exclaimed sympathetically. 'That's a real shame. Let's hope that you and Dr Kennedy have an easier ride for the rest of the trip.'

'I hope so,' she agreed, deeming it wiser not to mention that she might not be on board for the whole of the cruise.

She said goodbye and carried on but the thought of returning to England sooner than she'd planned was depressing. She'd had such high hopes for this job, seen it as a springboard to a whole new way of life. Now, once the agency had found someone to replace her, she would be right back to square one. It had taken a lot of courage to leave behind everything she knew and, despite what she'd told Liam yesterday, she wasn't sure if she would be able to do it a second time. However, there was no way that she could work with him when one night had caused such havoc.

Coffee and croissants were being served by the pool so Sophie had breakfast there rather than face the ordeal of sitting opposite Liam in the dining-room. She couldn't avoid him altogether, of course, but it would be best if she kept any contact between them on a strictly professional footing while she was on the ship.

She went back to her cabin afterwards to shower and change into her new uniform. The uniform at the Royal Memorial had consisted of baggy cotton trousers and an equally baggy V-necked top. However, the owners of the *Esmeralda* had opted for something more traditional.

Sophie had to admit that the short-sleeved white dress with its sea-green piping around the collar and cuffs was a lot more flattering.

She slid her feet into the smart white leather loafers that were part of the uniform then went to relieve Liam. It was just gone seven so he could hardly object. Sophie squared her shoulders as she paused outside the ward, wondering why she felt so nervous all of a sudden.

Liam means nothing to me now, she reminded herself as she turned the handle. Not only are we divorced but he's going to marry someone else. However, the moment she saw him, sitting slumped in the chair with his eyes closed and his dark hair falling over his forehead, her heart began to race. In that second Sophie knew that the bond between them hadn't been completely broken. There was still something left, although she had no idea what it was.

Surely after all the heartache he'd put her through she couldn't still feel anything for him?

Liam groaned. It felt as though every muscle in his body was aching. That was the trouble with these damned mattresses. Once the straw had flattened it was like sleeping on rock. He'd have to ask Benjamin to make him a new one…

He opened his eyes and blinked. He'd expected to see the bare mud walls of the hut where he'd slept for the past year but found himself gazing at smooth, sea-green plaster instead. His astonished gaze swept around the room as he took stock of the regulation hospital beds and the state-of-the-art monitoring equipment and he sighed. Things were definitely looking up if they'd managed to raise the standards at the clinic to this undreamed-of level…

'I thought you might want me to take over while you get ready for surgery.'

Liam jumped when a cool voice addressed him from the opposite side of the room. His gaze swivelled in that direction and he felt his heart give an almighty thump. Sophie! But what was *she* doing here? Had she come to ask him to go back home with her?

The thought barely had time to cross his mind before everything came rushing back. Liam just managed to stifle his groan of dismay when he realised his mistake. He wasn't in the middle of the African bush but on board a luxury liner cruising the Mediterranean. And as for Sophie wanting him to go home with her, well, the truth was that she couldn't wait to be rid of him, which was why she was going to hand in her notice that very day!

He shot to his feet, feeling like a complete and utter idiot. So maybe he *had* been half-asleep but was that any excuse? Surely Julia deserved better than a man whose thoughts continually returned to making up with his ex-wife?

'Why didn't you wake me earlier?' he demanded, self-disgust spilling over into anger. He glanced at his watch and frowned when he saw that it was only a few minutes past seven.

'Because I had no idea what time you wanted to be woken,' she replied stiffly, then ignored him as she set about doing the morning's obs.

Liam grimaced because it had been wrong to take out his anger on her. Sophie wasn't to blame because *he* kept having all these crazy thoughts. 'I'm sorry. I didn't mean to snap at you like that. I thought it was later than it is.'

'There's no need to apologise.'

She noted down the patient's BP, temperature and respiratory rates then checked how much fluid he'd passed.

Liam waited for a moment but it was obvious that she didn't intend to say anything else to make him feel better. Why should she when he'd acted like a total jerk?

'Maybe not, but I shouldn't have had a go at you like that,' he admitted, swallowing his pride. He searched for a way to explain his bad temper. What would she say if he confessed that he'd been angry at himself for thinking about her all the time? Would she be pleased, shocked or angry even? It was the fact that he had no idea how she would react that convinced him he couldn't possibly tell her the truth.

'You...um...caught me off guard,' he hedged, gritting his teeth when he realised how feeble that must have sounded.

'What do you mean?' She replaced the chart on the end of the bed and turned to look at him.

Liam felt a spasm shoot through him when he realised how lovely she looked that day. The tailored lines of the dress made the most of her slender figure, emphasising the high curve of her breasts and the narrowness of her waist. The spiky hairstyle had been brushed smooth that morning, silky wisps of blonde hair framing her face and drawing attention to her beautiful eyes.

She looked so fresh and beautiful that Liam felt his insides twist with desire before he sternly brought himself under control. He was trying to find a way to explain his error, not compound it by committing an even bigger one! He had to remember that he was going to marry Julia and not keep letting his thoughts stray all the time.

'I thought I was back in the clinic when I woke up.' He summoned a smile but it worried him that he needed to keep reminding himself about Julia all the time. Was he doing the right thing by marrying her or was he making a mistake?

'I was just congratulating myself on how well we'd done to raise the standards there when you spoke to me,' he explained hurriedly, because he couldn't deal with questions like that at the moment. 'It came as rather a nasty shock to discover that all this wonderful equipment hadn't suddenly materialised in the middle of the African bush!'

'And an even nastier shock to realise that I wasn't your fiancée, I expect.' She treated him to a chilly smile. 'I'm sorry to ruin all your dreams, Liam, although it's par for the course where you and I are concerned, isn't it?'

'Rubbish! That's nonsense, Sophie.'

'If you say so.'

It was obvious that she didn't believe him and Liam sighed. Maybe it was silly to make an issue out of this but he couldn't bear to think that she felt so badly about their past relationship.

'I do. OK, so maybe things didn't turn out how we'd planned when we got married, but it wasn't your fault.'

'Really? So you don't blame me for what happened to Zoë, then?'

Liam frowned when he heard the sudden catch in her voice. 'Why would I blame you? It wasn't your fault, Sophie. It was just one of those awful things that happen for no apparent reason.'

'You say that now, but at the time…' She broke off and bit her lip. Liam's hands clenched when he saw the struggle she was having not to cry. The urge to take her in his arms was so strong that it was a miracle he managed to resist. It was only the thought of the problems it could cause that gave him the strength to hold back.

'At the time…what? Tell me what you were going to say, sweetheart.'

The endearment slipped out without any conscious

thought and he saw her eyes fill with tears. Was she remembering all the times he'd used it in the past? he wondered with a heavy heart. He'd meant it, too, because Sophie had been his sweetheart from the day they'd met, and nobody could ever fill the place she'd always held in his heart. Not even Julia.

The thought shocked him to the core but he couldn't deal with it right then. Sophie was upset and he needed to find out what was troubling her. However, he was very aware that he would have to examine his feelings soon. He had to be one hundred per cent sure that he was doing the right thing before he embarked on a second marriage.

'What did you mean, Sophie?' he said gently. 'Please, tell me because I really want to know.'

'I...I thought you blamed me for what happened to Zoë.' She looked up and he could barely hide his dismay when he saw the anguish on her face. 'Maybe you were right to do so, too, because if I hadn't insisted on working then maybe she wouldn't have died. I...I've always wondered if that was the reason why you couldn't talk to me about what happened, because you felt it was all my fault.'

'No! How can you think such a thing?'

He crossed the room and took hold of her by the shoulders, forgetting his decision to keep his distance. To say that he was shocked would have been the biggest understatement of all time, but he was. How could Sophie imagine that he blamed *her* for the loss of their precious daughter?

'I have never blamed you, Sophie. Not once! Ever!' He gave her a gentle shake. 'Nobody could have prevented what happened. It wouldn't have made a scrap of difference if you'd given up work either. The consultant told you that at the time. It was just one of those terrible, tragic events that no one can explain.'

'I know what the consultant said but I keep going over everything I did.' She swallowed and Liam's heart ached when he saw the tears that trembled on her lashes. 'I wanted our baby so much and I can't help feeling that I was to blame because she died.'

'That's crazy and you know it is.' He ran his hands down her arms, desperate to convince her that she had nothing to reproach herself for. 'You did everything right, Sophie. You ate all the right things, went for your check-ups, attended antenatal classes... You did everything a woman should do when she's pregnant. I don't know why it had to happen but I do know it wasn't your fault.'

'So you didn't blame me?'

'No. Never.' His hands skimmed back up her arms and his breath caught when he felt the smoothness of her skin beneath his palms. He'd forgotten just how wonderfully soft her skin had always felt, he realised.

'Then why wouldn't you talk to me about Zoë after she died? Every time I tried to speak to you about her, you changed the subject, Liam.'

It was a relief when his hands encountered crisp cotton because it meant he could focus on the question. Liam knew he had to be truthful because it would be wrong to present himself in a better light by distorting the facts. He'd let Sophie down at a time when she'd desperately needed his support, and that was something he bitterly regretted.

'Because I didn't know how to deal with your grief when I was having such difficulty coping with my own,' he said simply.

'But we're both medical professionals. We've been

trained to help people work through their grief, for heaven's sake!'

'Yes, so we have. But no amount of training can prepare you when something like that happens, Sophie. It was like a bolt from the blue, wasn't it? It's little wonder that we found it impossible to cope.'

'I suppose so. You realise that Zoë would have been almost three by now? She'd have been running around, playing...'

Her voice broke and Liam groaned as he drew her into his arms because her pain was so hard to bear. He ran his hand over her hair, wishing there was a way to comfort her. How wrong he'd been to imagine that Sophie had put the past behind her. On the surface it might appear that she'd moved on but she was every bit as affected by it as he was. The memory of what they'd lost would bind them together for ever.

Afterwards, he wasn't sure if it had been that thought which had prompted him to kiss her. All he knew was that he suddenly found himself bending towards her. He felt her start of surprise when she realised what was happening but, oddly, she made no attempt to stop him. Maybe she needed this kiss just as much as he did.

Their mouths met softly, gently, and it felt like a homecoming. Liam was filled with a sense of wonder when his lips instantly recognised the taste and shape of hers. Two years had passed since they'd last kissed but the months faded into nothing as their mouths clung to each other.

Liam could feel a fullness in his heart, a sense of completion he'd never dreamed he would feel again. Kissing Sophie felt so right that it didn't even surprise him. He'd always felt this way about her, always known that she was the one person who could make him whole. When he held Sophie in his arms, he could solve the most difficult problems, find a way to right all the wrongs in the world. With her he was invincible. Without her, he was just a shell…

'No!'

He flinched when he heard the panic in her voice as she dragged her mouth away from his. He didn't try to hold on to her when she pushed him away. One glance was all it took to tell him that the last thing she wanted was him holding her, and his heart wept at the thought.

'I don't know what you think you're doing, Liam, but you're way out of order!'

She ran her hands over her face and Liam could see that she was trembling. But was it the fact that he'd had the temerity to kiss her or because she'd enjoyed it that was causing her such distress? All of a sudden it seemed vitally important that he found out the answer.

'You didn't exactly fight me off.'

'I…um… You took me by surprise.'

A little colour touched her cheeks but she met his eyes. 'That's the truth, Liam, so if you're harbouring any ideas that I'm still attracted to you, you can forget them. You made a fool out of me once and I most certainly won't give you the chance to do it a second time!'

His stomach twisted when he heard the contempt in her voice. It cut him to the quick that she could still believe he'd been unfaithful to her. Didn't she know how much he'd loved her and that having an affair with another woman had been out of the question?

Hurt and anger rose inside him but he knew how point-less it would be to protest his innocence right then. Sophie was in no mood to listen to reason and he really couldn't blame her. He *had* overstepped the mark even if she'd been a willing participant.

'Then all I can do is apologise.' He checked his watch,

deeming it wiser to bring matters to a speedy conclusion. 'I'd better go and get ready. Surgery starts at eight o'clock, I believe.'

'That's right. I'll get everything set up,' she replied stiffly.

'Thanks. That would be a big help.'

Liam didn't say anything more as he left the room and headed to his cabin, but he was bitterly aware of the mess he'd made of things. Charlie Henshaw knocked on the door while he was shaving to ask how Alexei was doing. Liam gave the steward a quick update on his friend's condition then asked Charlie if he would fetch him a cup of coffee. He really couldn't face the thought of making small talk over the breakfast table after what had happened.

He put on the white drill trousers and short-sleeved shirt which were the male version of the medical staff's uniform after the steward left. The cotton felt cold against his skin and he shivered. He'd taken this job in the hope that it would clarify his plans for the future but now it felt as though everything was up in the air. He was less certain than ever if he should marry Julia.

He stared into the mirror, seeing the doubts in his eyes. How could he go ahead and marry someone else when he felt so emotionally tied to Sophie?

CHAPTER FIVE

'DR KENNEDY is with a patient at the moment. If you'd care to take a seat, Mrs Hargreaves, he shouldn't be long.'

Sophie ushered the elderly woman towards a chair. A surprising number of people had turned up for the clinic that morning so they'd been kept busy from the moment they'd opened up. Most of the people they'd seen had been suffering from fairly minor ailments—coughs, colds, even a few complaining of sea-sickness despite how calm the weather was. They had been quickly dealt with and sent on their way.

Liam was presently examining a teenage boy, whose parents had insisted that he should see the doctor after he'd refused to eat any breakfast because he felt sick. Hopefully, it wouldn't turn out to be anything too serious, though.

'I hope you're right, Nurse.' Cynthia Hargreaves, a widow from Southampton, looked decidedly disgruntled as she sat down. 'I didn't expect to have to wait after I've paid so much money to come on this cruise. It's worse than the National Health Service back home!'

Sophie simply smiled, knowing from experience that it was best not to say anything. She went back to the consulting room and tapped on the door. Liam was sitting behind his desk and he glanced up when she went into the room. Sophie felt her heart miss a beat when she saw the brooding expression in his grey eyes.

Was he thinking about what had happened earlier? she wondered. Even though she bitterly regretted that kiss, she couldn't stop the tremor that coursed through her as she recalled how sweetly familiar Liam's lips had felt. For a few magical moments she'd forgotten about their differences and there was no point trying to pretend otherwise.

'Can you check if we have any soluble aspirin in the drugs cupboard, please, Sophie?'

'Of course.' Sophie hurriedly turned her attention to work and went to the cupboard. 'I take it these are for Michael Preston. Do you know what's wrong with him?'

'A hangover.' Liam grinned as he tilted back his chair. 'Turns out that young Michael helped himself to the contents of his parents' mini-bar while they were dancing the night away on deck. He's now paying the price for it.'

'Really?' Sophie couldn't help laughing. 'No wonder he couldn't face breakfast this morning. Let's hope it's taught him a lesson for the future.'

'Oh, I rather think it has. And if the perils of the demon drink haven't sunk in yet, they will once his father gets the bar bill.' Liam chuckled. 'From what Michael told me, he is going to have a lot of explaining to do!'

They both looked round as the screen parted and Michael appeared. Sophie hid her smile when she saw how pale the teenager looked. She popped a couple of soluble aspirins into a dispensing envelope, wrote the boy's name on it and handed it to him.

'There you are, Michael. Just dissolve these in a glass of water and they should help get rid of your headache.'

'Thanks,' Michael muttered sheepishly.

'Now, remember what I told you, young man. Drink plenty of fluids and stay out of the sun until you're feeling better.' Liam's tone was stern. 'There's no easy fix for a hangover so you'll just have to ride it out, I'm afraid. Take it as warning to behave more responsibly in future.'

'I will. Thanks, Dr Kennedy. You won't say anything

to my parents, though, will you?' Michael grimaced. 'I never wanted to come on this holiday in the first place. I wanted to go camping with my friends but Mum and Dad wouldn't hear of it. They insisted on us having a *family* holiday. I mean, it's bad enough being stuck with your parents for two whole weeks but if I have to put up with them lecturing me all the time then I'll probably throw myself overboard!'

'I won't say anything but they'll find out what you've been up to when it comes to paying the bill at the end of the trip,' Liam warned him. 'Your father will be charged for all the drinks you managed to consume last night.'

Michael groaned. 'They'll go totally ape when they find out! I'll be grounded for months. Being a teenager really sucks!'

He looked even more dejected as he left the room. Sophie sighed ruefully. 'There goes one very unhappy young man, although you couldn't blame his parents if they're angry when they find out what he's been up to. It must be a nightmare trying to deal with a teenager.'

'It must definitely test your patience, not that you or I ever gave our parents any cause for concern, of course.'

'Of course not!' Sophie pulled a face. 'You and I were the perfect teenagers and never gave our parents a moment's worry.'

'And if you believe that then you'll believe anything.' Liam laughed deeply. 'I must have pulled every stunt in the book when I was Michael's age. It's a wonder I made it past seventeen!'

'Really? I don't remember you mentioning that before,' Sophie said without thinking.

'No?' He shrugged. 'I probably decided not to tell you about my past misdemeanours in case it put you off.

Anyway, enough of all that. Is there anyone else waiting to be seen?'

'Yes. A Mrs Cynthia Hargreaves. Shall I show her in?'

Sophie hurried to the door when Liam nodded his assent. She ushered the woman into the room then stood to one side while Liam took down a very long and very detailed case history. Mrs Hargreaves seemed to have suffered from a vast number of ailments in recent months and it all took some time, but Sophie was glad of the respite because it gave her a chance to get her thoughts into order.

The way she'd slipped back into such easy familiarity with Liam was alarming after what had happened earlier that day. She would have to be more careful in future. She had no idea how long it would take the agency to find a replacement for her, but she and Liam would have to work together in the interim. She couldn't afford to get carried away by the memories they shared. It was the future that mattered now, what she would do once she left the ship, although building a new life for herself had never seemed a more daunting task.

She glanced at Liam and felt her heart ache because if things hadn't gone so drastically wrong then they might have been making those plans together. Her, Liam…and Zoë.

Liam was almost certain the chest pains Cynthia Hargreaves had experienced during the night had been caused by indigestion. Nonetheless, he decided not to take any chances. There was an ECG machine in the surgery so he did a heart tracing and was pleased when the results showed no abnormalities in its rhythm.

'Everything appears to be fine, Mrs Hargreaves. A nice

clear tracing which shows that your heart is behaving exactly as it should be doing.'

'But the pain was excruciating, Dr Kennedy! I was doubled up in agony.' Cynthia Hargreaves sounded put out rather than relieved by the news. 'Surely you don't think I'm making it up?'

'Certainly not,' Liam denied firmly, although he suspected that the woman's frequent bouts of illness were psychological rather than physiological. Cynthia Hargreaves had explained that she'd undergone a series of tests in the past twelve months for a wide variety of symptoms but that all had proved negative. She'd also mentioned that it was just over a year since her husband had died. Liam had gained the impression that she was lonely, which could explain her frequent visits to her GP.

'I'm quite sure you were in pain, Mrs Hargreaves, but I'm pleased to say that I cannot find anything wrong with your heart.' He chose his words with care. 'It could be that the rich food you ate last night caused the problem. Indigestion can be extremely distressing.'

'Indigestion! I was in agony, I tell you, absolute agony!'

'I appreciate that,' he put in quickly when he saw how upset she was by the suggestion. 'Indigestion can be really horrendous for anyone with a delicate constitution, and from what you've told me, it does seem as though you may need to be rather more careful about what you eat than most people.'

'Well, when you put it like that, Dr Kennedy, I can see what you mean. I've always had a delicate stomach.' Cynthia sounded much happier with that idea. 'Maybe I should have been a bit more careful last night.'

'I think it would be wise to watch what you're eating

for a few days.' Liam jotted some notes on a pad. He tore off the sheet and handed it to her.

'Just a few suggestions as to what you should avoid. Anything with a rich or spicy sauce, and dishes with a high fat content are the main culprits when it comes to triggering a severe bout of indigestion. Basically, I'd advise you to stick to fairly simple meals, although I know it won't be easy to refuse the wonderful food they serve on board this ship.'

'Oh, if it's for the benefit of my health then it won't be a problem, Dr Kennedy,' Cynthia said firmly. 'I'll be very careful about what I eat from now on. If there isn't anything suitable on the menu, I'll just have to ask the chef to prepare something especially for me.'

She smiled at him as she stood up. 'Thank you very much, Doctor. It's reassuring to know there is someone with your experience and sensitivity on board.'

'It was my pleasure, Mrs Hargreaves. I hope you enjoy the rest of your holiday.'

Liam hid his amusement as he escorted her to the door. He had a feeling the chef wasn't going to be too pleased if he was continually bombarded with special dietary requests. He sighed ruefully as he closed the door and glanced at Sophie.

'Ever had a feeling that you might have started something? Remind me to steer clear of the chef in future.'

'I'm sure the kitchen staff will cope,' she said flatly.

Liam frowned as he watched her push back the screens around the examination couch. It was obvious that something was troubling her but he wasn't sure if it was his place to ask what was wrong.

His mouth thinned because it was frustrating to have to monitor everything he said. He hadn't realised it would be so difficult to deal with this situation. He'd naïvely assumed they would be able to talk everything through after Sophie had got over her shock at seeing him, but things seemed to be getting worse rather than better and he only had himself to blame for that. He should *never* have kissed her that morning.

Liam's heart jerked so violently that it felt as though it was trying to leap right out of his chest. He'd done his damnedest to put what had happened out of his mind while he'd been taking surgery but now the patients had been safely dispatched he couldn't help thinking about it. Kissing Sophie had been a magical experience but he bitterly regretted it. It hadn't helped the situation one iota, plus it had filled his head with doubts about his relationship with Julia. Frankly, he didn't need the added stress. He'd taken this job to simplify his life, not make it even more complicated.

'I need to make that phone call to the agency. Would you mind if I did it now?'

'Of course I don't mind.' Liam steeled himself not to show how on edge he felt when Sophie turned to him. 'You don't need to ask my permission.'

'I can hardly go swanning off without telling you where I'll be, can I?' she countered, walking to the door. 'We're due to dock at Villefranche at eleven and I assume you'll need to make arrangements to have Alexei transferred to a hospital there.'

Liam frowned when he heard the challenge in her voice. Sophie was spoiling for a fight and it surprised him because she'd hated it on the rare occasions when they'd disagreed in the past. She'd always been the first to want to make up, not that he'd ever been unwilling...

He blanked out the thought of exactly *how* they had resolved their differences. Recalling how they had ended up in bed together would be foolish in the extreme. The only way was forward now, not back.

'I had a word with Mike Soames and it's all sorted out. He's just waiting for the company to e-mail him with the details of the hospital Alexei will be transferred to,' he explained. 'It shouldn't be long before we hear something so why don't you make that call while I check how Alexei's doing?'

'Fine. I shan't be long.'

Sophie left the consulting room and Liam followed her. He went straight to the ward. The patient was awake and Liam smiled at him as he went over to the bed.

'Good morning. How do you feel?'

'It hurts…' The young seaman grimaced as he touched his chest.

'I'll give you something for the pain after I've finished examining you,' Liam assured him. He checked the man's pulse, BP and temperature and nodded. 'So far so good. Now I'd just like to check that wound and see how it's doing.'

He pulled on a pair of latex gloves then carefully removed the light dressing he'd put over the wound. Alexei sucked in his breath when he saw the massive incision that ran right across his chest.

'It is so *big!*'

'It is.' Liam checked the sutures and nodded in satisfaction when he saw that the surrounding flesh was clean and healthy looking, with no sign of infection. 'That all looks fine. You were very lucky. Another few centimetres to the right and I doubt you'd be lying here now.'

'I was lucky because you were there to help me,' the man corrected. 'Thank you, Doctor. I shall never forget what you did for me last night. I owe you my life.'

'I'm glad I was able to help,' Liam replied sincerely.

He wrote up the chart and added analgesics then went to the office for the drugs. All in all, he was pleased with what they'd achieved last night, or he would have been if he didn't feel so downhearted at the thought of what Sophie was doing at that moment. He couldn't blame her for wanting to leave the ship but it hurt to know how eager she was to get away from him.

It hurt rather a lot.

It certainly hurt far more than it should have done.

Oh, hell!

Sophie sighed as she finished her call and hung up. The woman she'd spoken to at the agency had made it clear what a dim view she took of Sophie's request to leave the ship. There'd been mention of breach of contract and lawyers but Sophie had remained firm. In the end, the woman had told her that she would be in touch and hung up. Sophie had no idea how long it would take them to hire another nurse, but it appeared she might be staying on the ship rather longer than she'd hoped.

'Sophie! What a wonderful surprise. If I'd known you were coming to my office, I would have made sure I was here to meet you.'

'Hello, Yuri.'

She summoned a smile as the purser greeted her with undisguised enthusiasm. Although the paying passengers had telephones in their cabins, the crew had to use the purser's office to make any calls. She'd been relieved that Yuri hadn't been there when she'd asked to make a call to London. Although he was bound to find out that she was leaving, she preferred to avoid any awkward questions for as long as possible.

'I needed to make a phone call and your assistant helped me,' she explained, edging towards the door.

'There isn't a problem, I hope?' he said, neatly blocking her exit.

'No, no, everything's fine.' She glanced at her watch and feigned surprise. 'Oh, is that the time? I'd better get back.'

'I shall walk back with you,' Yuri offered immediately. 'I want to see how my friend Alexei is doing. I might not get a chance to speak to him once we reach the French coast and the passengers will need organising for the trip ashore.'

'He seems to be holding his own,' Sophie said, inwardly sighing as the purser followed her from the office. She'd been rather flattered at first when Yuri had shown an interest in her but now it just made her feel uncomfortable. She couldn't help wondering what Liam must think.

It was hard to hide her dismay when she realised how stupid that was. Liam was planning on getting married again so why should he care what she did?

'Good! That is excellent news, although I knew my friend would receive the very best of care with you to look after him, Sophie.'

Sophie decided it might be best not to respond to the compliment. She briskly led the way to the hospital bay, only pausing when they reached the office. 'Would you mind waiting here? I need to check with Dr Kennedy that it's all right for you to see your friend.'

'Of course.' Yuri treated her to a warm smile. 'I am happy to wait so long as I know that you will be coming back, Sophie.'

'Um. Right. Fine,' she burbled, somewhat unnerved by the ardent expression in his eyes. She hurried into the office and closed the door. Yuri seemed pleasant enough but she certainly didn't want him getting the wrong idea…

'Is there a problem with the agency?'

She jumped when Liam spoke, feeling her heart race when she looked round and found him studying her with concern. 'The agency?'

'You went to phone the agency about a replacement, didn't you?'

Her heart rate increased when he crossed the room and stopped in front of her because it seemed like a lifetime had passed since anyone had looked at her with such concern. It struck her then just how much she'd missed being able to turn to him for support.

'Is something wrong, Sophie? You seem upset.'

'I…I'm fine. I was just thinking about what the woman at the agency said.'

It was an effort to respond with a semblance of normality. Sophie took a steadying breath but it felt as though a giant hand was squeezing her heart. Liam had someone else who needed him now, another woman who could lean on him and turn to him for support. Even though she knew it was stupid, she couldn't help being jealous.

Liam frowned when he saw the myriad emotions that crossed Sophie's face because it was obvious that something was troubling her. He half reached towards her then stopped when he remembered what had happened earlier that day. One touch was all it had taken to trigger a chain of events that he didn't dare risk setting off again.

'Do I take it the person you spoke to at the agency wasn't pleased when you told her you wanted to leave?' he said thickly, struggling to suppress the memory of that kiss.

'You could say that.' She summoned a shaky smile. 'She threatened to sue me for breach of contract, although

I think it was more a way to frighten me into staying rather than a genuine threat.'

'It sounds nasty, though.' Liam couldn't hide his dismay. He couldn't help feeling responsible because if he hadn't taken this job then she would never have found herself in this difficult position.

'Oh, I'm sure it won't come to anything. Anyway, it's done now so there's no point worrying. They've agreed to find someone to replace me and that's the main thing.'

He felt his heart swell with sudden tenderness when he heard that. It was so typical of her to adopt that attitude. Sophie possessed the rare gift of finding something positive about the most difficult situation. It was one of the many things which had attracted him when they'd met, in fact, and it seemed she hadn't changed.

'I suppose so. Anyway, Alexei seems to be doing remarkably well, you'll be pleased to hear.' He quickly steered the conversation back onto safer ground because the thought unsettled him even more. Would it really be wise to start thinking about all the things he admired about her when his feelings were in such a state of flux? 'The wound is healing well and there's no sign of infection setting in.'

'Amazing when you consider the circumstances,' she agreed. 'You can perform an operation in the most sterile conditions possible and the patient will still contract an infection. Yet you performed this operation on the floor of a cabin and everything is fine.'

'There's a name for it, actually,' Liam said, wanting to lighten the mood because he couldn't deal with any more soul-searching. Examining how he felt about Sophie all the time was causing more harm than good.

'Really?' She looked up and despite his resolve he felt his insides melt when he saw the puzzlement in her beautiful blue eyes. 'I was a theatre nurse for five years and I never knew there was a medical term for this situation.'

'No?' He summoned a smile. 'That does surprise me. I thought you'd have come across it before.'

'I haven't.'

Sophie shook her head so that the soft blonde wisps of hair danced around her face. Liam felt a ripple run along his nerves and spread through his entire body. He was so very aware of her that it was sheer agony to not be able to touch her. But he had to remember that touching her was strictly off limits after this morning's little escapade.

'It's called Sod's Law,' he said huskily because he knew that he really shouldn't need any reminders. 'I'm sure you must have heard of it.'

'Sod's Law...?' She burst out laughing. 'You wretch! You had me convinced there was an actual medical term, too. I should have remembered how much you always love teasing people.'

'Moi?' He tried to look hurt. 'I'm absolutely gutted that you should accuse of me such a thing.'

'Oh, really? So what about the time you told that new houseman he was responsible for cleaning Theatre after each operation? He was absolutely horrified!'

'You were in on the joke as well,' he protested, laughing. 'So was everyone else who was in Theatre that day.'

'But you were the one to start it all off,' she pointed out. 'We were only following your lead. After all, you *were* in charge.'

'Mmm, I still think you were all accessories to the crime. Anyway, Pete saw the funny side in the end *and* it helped to break the ice. He was so terrified by the responsibility of having to deal with a real, live patient that he was thinking of giving up medicine,' he explained when her brows arched.

'I never knew that.' She frowned as she mulled it over. 'Is that why you pulled the stunt in the first place, Liam? So it would help Pete overcome his fears?'

'Yes. Surgery is one of the most demanding areas of medicine and it can be really over-awing for a newly qualified doctor.' He shrugged. 'Sometimes it helps to see there can be a lighter side to the job.'

'It worked for Pete because the last I heard, he'd taken a post as a surgical registrar in Glasgow.'

'I know. We still keep in touch. He came out to the clinic and did a stint there a few months ago, in fact. He has the makings of a first-rate surgeon, too.' Liam glanced round when there was a knock on the door. 'I wonder who that is.'

'Yuri!' Sophie clapped her hand to her mouth. 'I forgot he was waiting outside. He wanted to see how Alexei was doing.'

'I'd better have a word with him, then.'

Liam was suddenly glad of the interruption because reminiscing about the fun they'd had in the past was something they should avoid. Maybe Sophie had realised that, too, because her tone was far more distant all of a sudden.

'I'll make Alexei comfortable while you do that. I need to get him ready for the transfer to hospital.'

'Fine. Give me a shout when you've finished.'

'I shall.'

Liam took the purser into the office while Sophie carried out all the necessary tasks in preparation for the transfer ashore. He assured Yuri that his friend was out of danger and should be fine after a stay in hospital. Yuri was keen to see him so Liam took him to the ward then went to find Mike Soames and finalise the arrangements.

It turned out that there were all sorts of forms which

needed filling in so he took them back to the office and set to work. There was no sign of Sophie but he didn't check to see where she'd gone. They both needed a breathing space after the hectic night they'd had.

He sighed as he spread the forms across the desk because it wasn't work that was making the situation so stressful. Being around Sophie again was proving far more difficult than he'd imagined it would be.

CHAPTER SIX

THE ship anchored off Villefranche shortly before eleven that morning. Sophie went on deck to watch the tenders ferrying the passengers ashore. Some were going on a trip to Monte Carlo, a few miles further along the coast, whilst the rest intended to explore the town. She couldn't help wishing that she was going with them but she had work to do first.

'It shouldn't be long now. Mike Soames said we should be able to leave in about ten minutes' time.'

She glanced round when Liam joined her. 'Did Mike say how long it will take to reach the hospital once we're ashore?'

'Roughly half an hour. The company has booked Alexei into a private clinic just outside town. He'll stay there until the doctors decide he's fit enough to be flown home.'

'And what's going to happen about the other fellow—Grigorio, wasn't it?'

'That's right. He's being flown back to the Ukraine this morning and handed over to the authorities there,' Liam explained, leaning against the rail. 'Apparently, the captain decided not to involve the French police in case it resulted in the ship being delayed.'

'I don't imagine the passengers would be too happy if their holidays were ruined. Did you find out what the fight was about, by any chance?'

'According to Yuri, the two men are from the same town. Grigorio found out that Alexei had been seeing his

girlfriend and they had a blazing row.' He grimaced.
'Things progressed from there, apparently.'

'The course of true love,' she observed lightly.

'It never does run smoothly, does it?'

Sophie frowned when she heard the hollow note in his
voice. Was he thinking about what had happened to them,
perhaps? It was a relief when Mike Soames arrived just
then to tell them it was time to leave because she didn't
want to think about the past again.

They went back to the hospital and Sophie set about
checking that they had everything they needed for the
journey. Although an ambulance would meet them once
they reached shore, she didn't want to be caught out if
anything happened on the way. However, it was hard to
shut out the thought that Liam had sounded as though he
regretted the mess they'd made of their marriage.

She sighed as she zipped up the bag because it was far
too late for either of them to have regrets.

Getting Alexei into the tender proved to be a major under-
taking. The man was too ill to walk down the steps from
the ship and climb into the boat so he needed to be lowered into it on a stretcher. Mike had rigged up a pulley
and delegated half a dozen men to operate it, but it was
still a heart-stopping procedure.

Sophie waited in the boat with Liam while the stretcher
was lowered down to them. Fortunately, the sea was calm
that day and that helped. She couldn't begin to imagine
the problems they would have faced if the water had been
choppy. Liam grasped the end of the stretcher as soon as
it came within reach and guided it into the boat. Several
rows of seats had been removed but even so there was
barely enough room to fit it in. She heard Alexei groan

when the stretcher banged against the side of the boat before Liam managed to manoeuvre it into place.

'Can you check his pulse and BP?' Liam instructed, frowning as he took stock of the man's ashen face. 'I think I'll give him another shot of pethidine. It looks as though the last one might be wearing off.'

'Of course.'

Sophie quickly checked the man's pulse and blood pressure and was unsurprised to find both higher than they'd been first thing that morning. She reattached the line to the back of his hand then moved aside so that Liam could administer the drugs.

'This should help but the sooner we get him to hospital the happier I'll be.' He grimaced as he looked up at the ship towering above them. 'It's hardly ideal for a patient who's just undergone major surgery to find himself dangling fifty feet up in the air.'

'It certainly isn't.' She chuckled as she sat down. 'Coping with the odd little hiccup, like when the lifts stop working, is child's play compared to this.'

'Don't tell me they're still having problems with the lifts at the Royal Memorial?' Liam groaned when she nodded. 'I can't believe they haven't sorted things out after all this time!'

'The wheels of the NHS grind exceedingly slowly.'

'Rather like those wretched lifts!' His grey eyes gleamed with laughter as he sat down beside her. 'Do you remember when we got stuck on the way from Theatre that time?'

'Do I?' She rolled her eyes. 'It took me ages to live it down. I was teased unmercifully for months. Everyone seemed to think that we'd deliberately done something to stop the lift working!'

'I suppose it *did* look rather suspicious when we'd only just got back from our honeymoon.'

Sophie's heart thumped when she heard the warmly husky note in his voice. She knew he was thinking about the week they'd spent in Cornwall after they had married. It had been the depths of winter and the weather had been atrocious, but it hadn't mattered. They'd spent hours walking along the beach in the rain, oblivious to everything except each other. They had been so much in love that nothing could detract from their joy at being together.

She bent forward, making a great production of checking the drip while she struggled to get her emotions in check again. It hurt to remember how happy they had been once upon a time. She'd honestly believed they would be together for ever but she'd been wrong. The truth was that Liam simply hadn't loved her enough and she must never let herself forget that fact.

Liam bit back a sigh when he saw the shuttered expression on Sophie's face. It felt as though he was treading on eggshells every time he mentioned the past. He would have to be more careful, although it did seem to prove the point that they needed to talk. He would hate to think that her life would be forever blighted by the mistakes they'd made.

He looked round as Mike climbed into the tender, followed by a couple of the crew. There was barely enough room for them all, with the stretcher taking up so much space, but the men would be needed to carry Alexei ashore once they reached the harbour.

'All set?' Mike asked as one of the men started the motor.

'Ready when you are,' Liam confirmed.

Sophie quickly sat back in her seat as the boat surged

forwards. They left the shelter of the ship and he heard her gasp when the tender bounced as it struck a wave. He put out a steadying hand as she was jolted sideways in her seat.

'Sorry!' she exclaimed, quickly straightening.

'Don't worry. No harm done.'

He summoned a smile but it was difficult to ignore the shaft of awareness that had shot through him when her breast had brushed his arm. He focused on the view across the bay but it worried him that he should be so physically responsive to her. Sophie was a beautiful woman and it was only natural that he should be aware of that, but he'd never expected to feel this desire for her. Surely their past history should have damped down his ardour even if his commitment to Julia didn't seem to be making much difference to how he felt?

It was yet another question to add to all the others so that it was a relief when they reached the harbour and he had to concentrate on the practicalities of getting their patient ashore. Fortunately, Mike had the men well drilled so it all went quite smoothly. Once Alexei was safely on board the waiting ambulance, Liam checked the arrangements for getting back to the ship.

'We'll get a taxi back from the clinic,' he told Mike. 'I'm not sure how long it will take to sort out the formalities there so I can't give you an exact time when we'll need to be picked up.'

'Don't worry about it. We run a half-hourly service from shore to ship so that any passengers who get fed-up sightseeing can come back on board,' Mike explained. 'We set sail at sixteen-hundred hours so you'll have plenty of time to get back.'

'That's great. We'll see you later, then.'

Liam hurried back to the ambulance where Sophie was

waiting. Normally, he would have opted to sit in the back so he could monitor the patient during the journey, but he decided to sit in the cab and leave her to keep an eye on Alexei. The seaman was dozing now that the effects of the analgesics had kicked in and he didn't anticipate any problems. Nevertheless, he couldn't help feeling guilty as he explained that he'd sit up front to give her more room because he knew it was an excuse. The truth was that he wanted to avoid having to sit in such close proximity to her.

He sighed as he climbed into the cab. Would he have decided on this course of action if he'd realised the problems it was going to cause? Probably not. However, that didn't detract from the fact that he needed to tell Sophie the truth about what had gone on between him and Amanda two years ago. Once that issue had been resolved then they would both be able to get on with their lives, and that was what he wanted most of all. He certainly didn't want to spend the rest of his days in this emotional limbo!

It took just over an hour before the ambulance turned off the road into a tree-lined driveway. The driver pulled up in front of the clinic and switched off the engine. Liam quickly got out and helped him unload the stretcher so that within minutes they were wheeling Alexei inside. A nurse met them in the entrance hall and showed them to a bright and airy room where a doctor was waiting to receive them.

Liam busied himself with the formalities of handing over the patient into the French doctor's care. Fortunately, the other man spoke excellent English so he didn't have to dredge up his rusty, schoolboy French, but it all took some time. Sophie waited patiently at one side until they'd finished.

'*Merci.*' Liam shook the other doctor's hand then turned to her. 'That's it, then. Our bit is done.'

'And Alexei is in good hands, which is the main thing.' She led the way back to the reception area and paused uncertainly. 'How are we getting back to the ship?'

'I'll ask the receptionist if she can phone for a taxi for us.'

Liam went to the desk and laboriously explained in halting French that they needed a taxi to take them back to Villefranche. He smiled ruefully when the woman replied in perfect English that she would phone for one immediately. '*Merci, madame.*'

He went back to Sophie. 'It's all arranged. I've no idea how long it will take for the taxi to get here so d'you want to wait in here until it arrives or outside?'

'Outside,' she said promptly. 'It's such a glorious day and it's a shame to waste it.'

They went outside and Liam spotted a bench close to the entrance. 'We can sit here, if you like. Hopefully, the taxi won't be too long getting here.'

'There's no rush. I'm more than happy to soak up some of this wonderful sunshine.'

Liam laughed as she sat on the bench and tipped her face up to the sun. 'You'll regret it if you get burned. You always used to complain that you never tanned but just went lobster-red.'

'Unlike you who only had to see the faintest glimmer of sunshine and ended up as brown as toast.' She shaded her eyes and studied him thoughtfully. 'In fact, you're browner than I've ever seen you. It must be from working abroad for all that time.'

'Probably.' He hurriedly sat down, hoping she couldn't tell how unsettled he felt when she stared at him like that. Shivers were racing through him, making his whole body tingle with awareness, and it was the last thing he needed at the present time.

'I don't know if I could cope with that type of climate.' Fortunately, she didn't appear to have noticed anything amiss as she settled back and closed her eyes. 'I love the sun but I imagine it must be very uncomfortable having to work in all that heat.'

'It does get difficult.' He felt himself relax as they moved onto a relatively safe topic. 'Most days the temperature was well over a hundred and it took some getting used to, I have to admit.'

'I suppose you have to give yourself time to adapt to the conditions. Julia must be used to the heat by now. You said that she'd been working overseas ever since she qualified?'

'That's right,' he agreed shortly, hoping that Sophie wouldn't ask him anything else. Maybe it was silly but it felt wrong to discuss Julia with her, as though he were committing some sort of transgression by talking about another woman.

'Why did she choose to do that kind of work? It's not exactly the easy option, is it?'

'She told me that she wanted to see something of the world, which is why she signed on with the aid agency.'

It was an effort to keep his tone level because that thought had struck far too deeply. Surely he should be more concerned about Julia's feelings rather than Sophie's, and yet he couldn't put his hand on his heart and swear that was the case.

'So she's the adventurous type—unlike me. I was always happiest at home.' She laughed wryly. 'Not that I'm saying I'm boring or anything!'

'It isn't boring to know what you want from life. Not everyone can be the adventurous sort.'

'I never realised that you were until you told me where you'd been working.'

'I was always keen to travel when I was younger. It just didn't happen.'

'Because you met me?' She opened her eyes and looked at him. 'I'm right, aren't I, Liam? If you hadn't met me then you might have gone abroad earlier in your career.'

'Possibly,' he hedged, not wanting to make an issue out of it.

'You mean probably, don't you?' An expression of pain crossed her face. 'I never realised I was holding you back.'

'You weren't, not the way you mean, at any rate.'

He turned to face her, unsure why it seemed so important that she should believe him. 'All right, so maybe I *did* change my mind about working abroad after I met you, but I was more than happy with the decision I made. I certainly didn't regret it.'

'No?'

He sighed when he heard the scepticism in her voice. 'No,' he stated firmly. 'I never once wished that I'd done things differently and that's the truth.'

'All right, I believe you, but I'm sure there must have been times when you wished I was more adventurous.'

'I didn't. I loved you just the way you were.'

The words slipped out before he could stop them and Liam felt the blood drum through his veins when he realised what he'd said. He didn't dare look at her because he wasn't sure what would happen if he did. He *had* loved her, so much that it had broken his heart when she'd told him she wanted a divorce. But what was the point of telling her that now?

It was a relief when the sound of an engine announced

the arrival of their taxi. Liam got up and flagged it down. He told the driver where to take them then opened the door for her to get in.

'Thank you.'

Sophie carefully avoided looking at him as she took her seat. He climbed in beside her and sat stiffly as they were whisked back to the town. Sophie didn't say a word all the way there. She stared out of the window, seemingly engrossed by the view of pine-clad hills.

Liam was glad because he didn't think he could have managed to chat about trivialities after that admission he'd made. He sighed as he thought about what had happened in the past two days. He simply hadn't been prepared for the maelstrom of emotions he'd experienced since he'd seen Sophie again. Even though he knew it was wrong, he couldn't help comparing how he'd felt about her to how he felt about Julia now. Of course they were two completely different people so his feelings were bound to be different...different but equally strong.

He frowned because that was the real crux of the problem, wasn't it? He wasn't sure that what he felt for Julia could ever compare to how he'd felt about Sophie. His love for her had been all-encompassing. It had been the colour in his life, the air he breathed, his reason for living. He just didn't feel that way about Julia and wasn't sure that he ever would. But if that was the case, how could he go ahead and marry her? Surely Julia deserved more than he could give her, someone who would love her with whole-hearted devotion? Maybe the only honourable thing he could do was to let her go, but he needed to be sure first that he wasn't making another mistake.

He sighed again because there was no guarantee he would get it right this time, was there?

* * *

It was the Captain's Dinner that night and the dress code was strictly formal. Sophie took great care getting ready although her heart really wasn't in it. She and Liam were expected to attend as part of their duties but if there'd been a way to avoid going to the dinner, she would have made her excuses.

The thought of spending more time with Liam after what had happened that afternoon filled her with dread. Maybe it was wrong to get upset because he'd told her how much he'd loved her but she couldn't help it. For the past two years she'd blamed him for the fact their marriage had ended, but now she couldn't stop wondering if she'd been at fault in some way. What had she done to make him *stop* loving her?

She tried to push the question to the back of her mind as she finished getting ready. She was expected to act as one of the hosts during the evening and she couldn't afford to let herself get so distracted that she made a complete mess of things. Stepping in front of the mirror, she checked that her dress really was suitable for the occasion.

Made from filmy layers of silver-grey chiffon, it was the most sophisticated dress she'd ever owned. The softly draped bodice was held in place by spaghetti-thin straps which left her shoulders bare, whilst the split in the front of the skirt revealed glimpses of her slender thighs whenever she moved. She knew that it suited her but she couldn't help wondering if it was a little too daring. After all, she was part of the crew, not one of the passengers, and she didn't want to give people the wrong impression…

She sighed because what she really meant was that she didn't want to give *Liam* the wrong impression, but why should she imagine that he'd care how she looked? He'd made it clear that although he might have loved her once upon a time, he didn't harbour such feelings for her now.

It was upsetting to have to face that fact so Sophie blocked it from her mind as she spritzed herself with perfume then found her evening bag. A last check to see that her hair was all right and she was ready to face whatever the evening would bring, although she sincerely hoped it wouldn't be anything too stressful.

There was a crowd gathered in the Ocean View Bar when she arrived. Passengers were already queuing up to be introduced to the captain and Sophie wasn't sure whether she should join them or make her way straight through to the dining room. She breathed a sigh of relief when she saw Mike Soames heading her way.

'Just the person I need. Do I have to line up for the introductions or can I go straight in?'

'I'm sure the captain would like to meet you, Sophie, but there's no need to line up. Let me give Liam a shout and I'll take you both through to meet him.'

Mike swung round and waved to someone across the room before she could say anything and her breath caught when she spotted Liam heading towards them. He was wearing a white dinner jacket in honour of the occasion and she couldn't help thinking how much the formal clothes suited him. The cut of the jacket emphasised the width of his shoulders whilst the colour set off his tan. He'd brushed his dark brown hair straight back from his forehead but one wayward strand had fallen over his left eyebrow, lending him a rakish air that was extremely sexy.

Sophie noticed several women turn to look at him and her heart suddenly began to race. She wasn't sure if it was seeing how other people reacted that made her look at him afresh but she was suddenly struck by how tall he was, how handsome, how very virile and masculine. In that moment she knew that although their marriage might have ended the attraction she'd always felt for him was still very much alive.

Liam still possessed the power to make her want him as no other man had ever done, and the thought filled her with fear. She couldn't afford to fall in love with him all over again!

Liam felt a sudden tightness in his chest. Sophie was staring at him and he wasn't sure what he could see in her eyes but it had the most unnerving effect. It was as though his body had forgotten how to function all of a sudden. His heart had slowed to a crawl, his blood seemed to be stagnating in his veins and as for his breathing…

Well!

In-out, he instructed himself desperately. Take a breath then let it out again. He'd been doing it for thirty-three years but the simple act of getting oxygen into his lungs had never seemed a more daunting task.

He sucked in an extra-large lungful, choked and swiftly recovered, but it wasn't easy to pretend everything was normal. Was it his imagination or were the vibes in the air making everyone else's nerves twang like badly plucked guitar strings? He glanced at Mike but the other man seemed oblivious to what was happening right under his nose.

'Bit of a scrum tonight,' Mike observed cheerfully. 'It's always the same when we have one of these dinners. Everyone wants to have their photo taken with the captain.'

'I…um…yes. I suppose they do.' Liam tried to smile even though he couldn't actually *feel* his lips. He inhaled again in the hope that a little more oxygen might gee everything up, and groaned when the delicious fragrance of Sophie's perfume wafted up his nostrils and undid all his good work.

'Are you all right, Liam?'

The concern in her voice would have been music to his ears if he hadn't felt so wretched. He could barely breathe, his heart had virtually given up beating and it was best not to mention what his nerves were doing. How could he honestly claim to be fine in these circumstances?

'I...um...'

'Quick. Let's get you both in while there's a bit of a lull.'

Mike grasped them by the arms and hustled them towards the dining-room. Liam might have protested if he'd had the wherewithal to summon up the necessary reserves. He really needed a few minutes' grace before he could hope to function like the halfway intelligent being he was supposed to be, but Mike obviously didn't intend to let the opportunity pass them by.

'Captain Masters, may I present Dr Liam Kennedy and Miss Sophie Patterson.' Mike quickly introduced them to the dignified, silver-haired man standing beside the doorway to the dining-room.

'Delighted to meet you both.' Captain Masters shook their hands. 'And may I say how much I appreciate everything you did last night, Dr Kennedy. Your prompt actions undoubtedly saved that young man's life.'

'It was a pleasure,' Liam murmured, gritting his teeth when he realised how inane it probably sounded to describe open-heart surgery as a pleasure.

Fortunately, the captain didn't appear to think it strange as he thanked Sophie for her help as well. Liam edged away because he couldn't face the thought of making conversation with only a tenth of his brain cells functioning.

Thankfully, the queue had started to build up again so the captain didn't try to detain them. Liam strode into the dining-room and quickly consulted the table plan to find out where he would be sitting. He rolled his eyes in despair when he discovered that he and Sophie were on the same table.

'Table 15,' he told her tersely when she stopped to check the plan. 'We're seated together.'

'Oh, I see. Right. Fine.'

She didn't sound as though it was fine and his jaws snapped together with an audible click. Did she have to make it so abundantly clear that she hated the thought of spending the evening with him?

He led the way to their table and punctiliously drew out her chair because he didn't intend to give her an opening to criticise his manners, or anything else for that matter. He would be politeness itself, cool, calm, collected…

She slid into the seat and he almost leapt out of his skin when her bare shoulder brushed his knuckles. He could feel the hardness of the wood beneath his palms and the softness of her skin against his fingers and his sluggish heart suddenly zipped into overdrive.

Liam took his seat, wondering what he was going to do. If he'd had a choice, then he would have got up and left, but it wasn't an option when he was expected to act as a host that evening. At any rate, it wouldn't solve his biggest problem.

He had to decide *why* he felt this way. It wasn't just the repercussions it could have on his relationship with Julia—he needed to be clear in his own mind about his feelings. He had firmly believed that he'd got over Sophie and that all he needed to do was to sort out their past mistakes and he could move on, but it wasn't that simple any longer.

He glanced at her and felt his heart ache with a sudden, knifing pain. Relegating Sophie to the past might not be the solution, after all.

CHAPTER SEVEN

DINNER was a nightmare. Sophie was so conscious of Liam sitting across the table from her that she could barely eat. Every time she looked up, he seemed to be watching her.

She toyed with her food, eating a mouthful of this, a sliver of that, all the time longing for the meal to end so she could escape. Fortunately, no one seemed to notice her lack of appetite because they were too busy enjoying themselves. Gloria and Randolph Walters were on their table again and they kept the conversation flowing.

'Tell me, Dr Kennedy, what made you decide to take a job on board this ship?' Gloria smiled at Liam. 'Was it the opportunity to travel that attracted you most?'

'Not really. I'd been working overseas and had originally decided to spend some time back home in the UK,' Liam explained. 'This job just came up and it fitted in with my plans so I took it. It was as simple as that.'

Sophie picked up her glass, thinking how odd it was that fate had intervened like that. If Dr Hampson hadn't retired then Liam would never have been able to follow her onto the ship. Would he have tried to get in touch with her some other way? she found herself wondering, but it was impossible to say. It was strangely unsettling to realise that she might never have seen him again so that it was an effort to concentrate when Gloria asked her the same question.

'I wanted a complete change of scene,' she replied truthfully. 'I was in a bit of a rut and decided this job would be perfect. I'd get to see something of the world while I made up my mind what I wanted to do with the rest of my life.'

She put her glass back on the table and glanced at Liam, unable to resist seeing what he thought about her answer. She felt her heart lurch when she saw the frown on his handsome face. Why did she have a feeling that he was upset by what she'd said?

The conversation moved on but it was difficult to dismiss the idea even though she tried her best to join in. She deliberately avoided looking at Liam again but it didn't mean she wasn't acutely aware of him. It was a relief when the meal ended and their waiter announced that coffee would be served in the Ocean View lounge.

Sophie quickly stood up, hoping this would be her chance to escape, but Randolph forestalled her. He offered her his arm with old-world gallantry.

'Allow me, my dear.'

Sophie hesitated but there was no way that she wanted to offend the elderly man. She slid her hand through his arm, her heart sinking when she saw that Liam was escorting Gloria into the lounge. It seemed they were destined to spend even more time together.

'Thank you, Mr Walters.'

'Call me Randolph. Please.' He smiled at her. 'I won't feel quite so old then!'

She laughed, hoping he couldn't tell how on edge she felt as he escorted her to a table by the window where his wife and Liam were already sitting. 'I'd be delighted, Randolph. Thank you.'

She accepted the cup of coffee Gloria poured for her and added milk and sugar then passed the sugar basin to Randolph who shook his head.

'Let Dr Kennedy have it first.'

'Oh, Liam doesn't take sugar,' she said without think-ing, then flushed when she realised how revealing that had been.

'It's taken me the best part of forty years to work out that Gloria doesn't take cream in her coffee.' Randolph winked at her. 'You must be a fast study, my dear.'

'I...um... Yes.' Sophie summoned a smile but it was disconcerting to realise how easily she'd forgotten that she and Liam were supposed to have only just met. She sipped her coffee, thinking how hard it was to perpetuate a lie. You needed to be constantly on your guard otherwise the truth would slip out.

She frowned because she simply couldn't imagine Liam being able to maintain a lie. He'd always been too open and honest to resort to subterfuge. Nevertheless, he'd lied about his relationship with Amanda, hadn't he? He'd not only told her he'd been working when he'd been seeing the other woman, but he'd also told her that he hadn't had an affair when she'd challenged him. At the time she'd been too hurt and angry to really think about it, but all of a sudden she found herself wondering how Liam had managed to keep on telling all those lies...

Unless he hadn't been lying to her, of course.

She put the cup on the table because her hands were trembling and she was afraid she might drop it. It felt as though her head was going to burst from all the thoughts that were crowding into it. What if Liam *had* been telling her the truth all along and she just hadn't believed him? She'd been so heartbroken after Zoë had died that she'd found it impossible to deal rationally with the thought that he had betrayed her. She hadn't even considered the fact that it might have been a silly misunderstanding. Oh, he had tried to explain but she had refused to listen because it had been too much to cope with on top of everything else. But maybe she should have listened, should have tried to understand, should have had more *faith* in him!

Sophie bit her lip because there was no way she could close her mind to the truth. Liam had told her that very day how much he'd loved her and she had wondered what had caused his feelings to change, so was this the answer? Had it been her own lack of trust that had destroyed his love for her?

Liam checked his watch, wondering how soon he could make his exit without appearing rude. He'd been on pins all through dinner in case he made a fool of himself. Sitting opposite Sophie had been both a torment and a delight—a delight because she'd been close enough to see and hear her, and a torment because he'd been unable to touch her.

Sophie was strictly off-limits, he reminded himself. Forbidden. *Verboten.* If he told himself often enough then maybe—just *maybe*—it would sink in.

'Are you two young people going dancing tonight?'

'No!'

'No!' Liam summoned a smile when he saw Gloria's surprise as both he and Sophie answered with a resounding negative. 'I think that's a no from both of us. I expect Sophie is as worn out as I am after last night.'

'Of course.' Gloria patted his arm. 'Randolph told me that you two had to deal with some sort of emergency. Still, there will be plenty more nights when you'll be able to have fun, won't there?'

'I expect so.' Liam hurriedly stood up because that comment had hit a nerve. Sophie wouldn't have many more nights to enjoy herself on the ship and it was all his fault. He dredged up a smile for the benefit of the elderly couple but he couldn't help feeling bad about ruining her plans.

'I hope you won't think me rude but I'm going to have an early night and try to catch up on some of the sleep I missed.'

'That sounds like a very sensible idea,' Gloria assured him. 'We'll see you tomorrow at breakfast, I expect.'

'I think I'll have an early night as well,' Sophie said, quickly following suit. She shook her head when Randolph went to rise. 'No, please, don't get up. Enjoy the rest of your evening.'

She led the way across the room and Liam slowly followed, hoping that he might be able to avoid walking back to their cabins with her if he dallied long enough. Maybe it was cowardly but he didn't trust himself not to say the wrong thing after what had just happened. He was bitterly aware that Sophie could have carried on with her plans if he hadn't taken this job and he couldn't help feeling guilty about the problems he'd caused for her.

Fortunately, Mike stopped him on the way out to ask if Liam would consider joining him for a game of squash the following day, so that provided a welcome delay. Liam spent several minutes sorting out the arrangements so that it came as a surprise when he discovered that Sophie had waited outside for him.

'Sorry about that. Mike wanted to know if I'd play squash with him,' he explained, wondering what she wanted to speak to him about. There was obviously something on her mind because he could see how on edge she looked, and his heart fitted in an extra couple of beats as he wondered what was wrong.

'So you still play?'

'Occasionally.' He shrugged as they crossed the foyer with its gleaming Italian marble floor and crystal chandeliers. 'I've not had much opportunity to play in the past year. Squash courts are non-existent where I was working.'

'I suppose they are.' She sounded distracted and Liam sighed as he put his hand on her arm and turned her to face him.

'What is it, Sophie? I can tell something is worrying you.'

'There is...' She stopped as a group of people came out of the bar. One of the men had a handful of party poppers and Liam felt her jump when there was a loud bang. He nodded towards the deck.

'Do you want to go outside? It should be a bit quieter out there.'

'Yes, if you don't mind.'

She didn't say anything else as she swiftly made her way to the doors that led to the promenade deck. Liam followed her with his heart racing. Something was definitely wrong and he couldn't help feeling nervous, even though he had no idea what it was.

They made their way to a secluded spot near the prow of the ship and stopped. There was a light breeze blowing that night and he saw her smooth down her dress when the wind tugged playfully at the delicate chiffon layers. He turned and stared out to sea, trying to prepare himself, but it was hard to know how he was going to react to whatever Sophie wanted to tell him.

'I need to ask you something, Liam.'

He stiffened when he heard the tension in her voice. 'I see.'

'But before I do, will you promise me that you'll tell me the truth?'

She turned to look at him and his heart ached when he

saw the anguish in her eyes. He knew then that he would promise her the world if it would make her feel better.

'Yes. I promise,' he replied thickly.

'All right, then…did you have an affair with Amanda?'

Sophie could feel a tremor working its way through her body and gripped hold of the handrail for support. She knew it was a risk to ask Liam that but she had to know the truth…

'No. I didn't.'

His voice was so flat and unemotional that it took a moment for the actual words to sink in. Sophie bit her lip as a wave of sickness washed over her but she couldn't afford to break down when she had to clear up this misunderstanding.

'And those times when you were supposed to be working late?' she said in a dull little voice.

'That was exactly what I was doing. I was at the hospital each time.'

This time his voice grated, although whether from anger or frustration at having to answer her questions, she had no idea. She turned and stared at the black swell of the waves again while her mind struggled to adjust to what she'd just learned.

Liam hadn't had an affair.

All those hours he'd spent away from home he'd been working.

She had made the most dreadful mistake by not believing him.

'The only time I wasn't working was the night I spent at Amanda's flat. And absolutely nothing happened that night either.'

She had to force herself to concentrate when he continued because the throbbing ache inside her was making her feel sick. 'What made you decide to stay the night at her flat in the first place?'

'Because I was too drunk to make my way home.' He shrugged when she glanced at him in surprise but she saw the regret in his eyes. It made her feel even worse because he had nothing to reproach himself for.

'All the heartache I'd been bottling up over Zoë just caught up with me and I went out and got seriously drunk. If Amanda hadn't offered me a bed, I would have spent the night on the streets. She took me home and let me sleep on her couch. That was all there was to it.'

'Why didn't you tell me at the time?'

'Because I was too ashamed of what I'd done,' he replied with heart-wrenching honesty. 'You assumed I'd been working so I left it at that.'

'And that's how the story about you two having an affair must have started,' she said hollowly. 'Someone found out that you'd spent the night at Amanda's flat and put two and two together.'

'Yes. I don't know who started it. Probably one of Amanda's friends, having a bit of fun. But I never had an affair with Amanda or with anyone else.'

She heard him take a deep breath and suddenly wished with all her heart that she could stop him saying anything else. It was bad enough having to deal with what she'd learned so far without adding to her guilt.

'I loved you, Sophie. You and Zoë were the only people who really mattered to me. I know you didn't believe me at the time, but I hope you believe me now so we can try to put it all behind us at last.'

He took her hands and his fingers were icy cold despite the warmth of the night. 'That's the reason why I was so desperate to see you again. I need to draw a line under the past and make a fresh start.'

He didn't say anything else but he didn't need to because Sophie understood what he meant. He wanted to draw that line so that he could make a fresh start with *Julia*.

Pain ripped through her and she bit her lip because it would be far too easy to say something she would regret. It was too late to apologise for her blindness, her stubbornness, her...her lack of trust! Liam loved someone else now, a woman who would never make the mistakes *she'd* made or suffer the consequences. Julia would give him the happiness he deserved and she wouldn't say anything to make him feel bad about it.

'Thank you. I appreciate your honesty, Liam. I'm only sorry...' She stopped because there must be no more talk of the past from now on. 'I'm sure you know what I mean so let's leave it at that.'

She reached up and kissed him lightly on the cheek and it was all she could do to step back when she ached to throw her arms around him and beg his forgiveness.

'I hope that you and Julia will be very happy' she said huskily, her voice thick with unshed tears. 'You deserve to be, Liam. Really you do.'

He didn't try to stop her when she moved away. He didn't call her name or say anything, in fact. Maybe he'd already started to cut her out of his life now they'd sorted out their past misunderstandings.

Sophie went to her cabin and sank down on the bed. There was a hollow feeling inside her, a sense of loss so deep that it felt as though the world had come to an end. It was stupid, really, because the life she'd had with Liam had ended a long time ago, but even though her mind understood that, her heart couldn't seem to accept it. For some reason it felt as though she'd just lost him all over again.

* * *

'If you could try to raise your arm for me, Mr Jenkins…
That's fine. I can tell it's uncomfortable so just relax.'

Liam sat down behind the desk. It was the fifth day of
the cruise and once again a number of people had turned
up for surgery that morning. The ship wasn't due to dock
until the following day and he'd discovered that the number of patients he saw fluctuated according to their sched-
ule.

If they were due in port early in the day then people
put up with their ailments while they went sightseeing.
However, if they weren't due to dock until the evening,
they visited the surgery. At least he had an idea of what
to expect, which was something. It helped to have some
structure to his working life when his private one seemed
to be in such turmoil.

'Do you have any idea what's wrong with me, Dr
Kennedy?' Alan Jenkins, a retired company director from
London, grimaced as he rotated his left shoulder. 'This
shoulder's been giving me gyp for a couple of weeks now.
I've tried taking paracetamol for the pain but it doesn't
seem to help very much.'

'I'm afraid you're suffering from supraspinatus syndrome, or painful arc syndrome if you prefer a less fancy
name.'

Liam summoned a smile but it was difficult to shake
off the feeling of frustration which had been his constant
companion since the night he and Sophie had spoken
about the past. That had been two days ago and he hadn't
tried broaching the subject again because she hadn't given
him an opportunity to do so. She was always pleasant,
always professional while they were in work, but extremely distant. It was as though she had deliberately
erased their past relationship from her mind.

'So what exactly is painful arc syndrome, Dr Kennedy?'

'It's caused by inflammation of a tendon or a bursa—a fluid-filled pad that acts as a cushion around a joint.' Liam hastily refocused his thoughts on work. 'In your case, pain occurs when the arm is raised away from the body and the tendon or bursa is squeezed between the top of the shoulder-blade and the upper arm bone.'

'But what's caused this inflammation, Doctor?' Margaret Jenkins, Alan's wife, put in. 'Alan has always been so healthy. He's *never* had a problem like this before.'

'Usually inflammation is caused by pressure or repeated strain being put on the affected area. Housemaid's knee and tennis elbow are both prime examples.'

'How about golf?' Margaret shot a speaking look at her husband. 'Alan has taken up golf since he retired and he's on the golf course morning, noon and night. He only agreed to come on this cruise after he found out there was a driving range on board!'

Liam smiled. 'Well, I have to say it does sound like a possible cause. Each time your husband swings a golf club he's putting more strain on the affected area.'

'See. I told you that you were spending too much time at the club!' Margaret glared at her husband. 'The holiday is going to be completely ruined now by you complaining that you're in pain all the time.'

'I can give your husband an injection to ease the pain,' Liam cut in, hoping to restore harmony. 'Corticosteroids will make a huge difference so long as you rest your arm, of course, Mr Jenkins.'

'Oh, he'll rest it all right.' Margaret stood up. 'I'm going to tell the steward to stow those wretched golf clubs in the hold. And you just be grateful that I don't tell him to throw them overboard!'

Alan sighed as his wife left the room. 'Looks as though I'm in the doghouse.'

'Sorry,' Liam apologised wryly.

'Not your fault, Doctor. You're only doing your job and I'll be glad to have an end to this pain.' Alan chuckled. 'Anyway, it's a husband's place to be in the wrong, isn't it?'

Liam simply smiled as he got up to fetch the drugs. He'd been wrong not to make Sophie listen two years ago when he'd tried to tell her the truth, and he'd paid the price for it, too. If they had talked then they might never have got divorced.

It was odd how painful he found that thought, bearing in mind that he should be far more concerned about his future plans. He gave Alan the injection then told him to see Sophie on his way out so she could explain about the billing arrangements. The passengers had to pay for any treatment they received whilst they were on board the ship, but as they were covered by insurance it didn't appear to present a problem.

He took Alan out to the front office, fixing a neutral expression on his face when Sophie looked up. So far as she was concerned, they had sorted everything out and it would be wrong to let her see that the mistakes he'd made in the past still plagued him.

'Would you explain to Mr Jenkins about the charges, please, Sophie?'

'Of course.' She treated him to a smile which was neither overly warm nor excessively chilly and Liam swallowed his sigh. If only he could accept what had happened as she seemed to have done then maybe he would feel better about it.

He went back to his office to await the next patient. There was still half an hour left before surgery was due to end and someone might turn up. Sitting down at his desk, he thought about what had happened. Even though he didn't feel that he'd handled the situation very well, at least he'd managed to solve some of his problems. Now it was time to start making plans. Julia was due to return to England in September, by which time he would have completed his contract on board the *Esmeralda*. Maybe they should think about setting the date for their wedding then? After all, there was nothing to stop them...

Apart from the fact that he still wasn't sure if it was what he wanted. Could he *really* see himself and Julia spending the next forty odd years together?

Liam frowned as he tried to picture their future life together. Of course, it might have helped if he'd had an idea where they would be living but he hadn't. They might decide to settle in England, go back to Africa or even start afresh somewhere entirely different. There was absolutely no point dreaming about a cottage with roses around the door and a stream at the bottom of the garden.

His heart sank when it struck him that it had been the dream he and Sophie had shared. They'd wanted a cottage in the country with a huge garden where their children could play in safety. They'd decided to have three and had agreed that it didn't matter if they were boys or girls.

He frowned again. He and Julia had never discussed issues like where they would live and how many children they wanted. He had no idea if she even wanted a family because the subject simply hadn't arisen. Their conversations had centred on the clinic and the constant problems of keeping it running with so few resources.

If he was being completely honest then he actually knew very little about her. He had no idea what her tastes were in music or films, if she enjoyed holidays by the sea or preferred to spend her time in the country. Their work had drawn them together—a shared desire to do their very best for the people they treated. But was it the only thing they had in common?

Liam felt a sudden tightness in his chest as panic hit him. He'd accepted that he didn't love Julia the way he'd loved Sophie but did he love her at all? He needed to make up his mind about that before he went any further.

CHAPTER EIGHT

A HEAT wave had hit Malta by the time the *Esmeralda* docked at Valletta on the Saturday morning. Temperatures had soared to over a hundred degrees during the previous week and everyone who was planning to go ashore had been warned to use a high-factor sunscreen and drink plenty of bottled water.

Sophie packed a small haversack with everything she would need and left it on her bunk. Once morning surgery was over she had the rest of the day free and she intended to make the most of it.

She'd tried not to let Liam see how upset she'd been at the thought of the mess she'd made of things, but the strain of constantly being on her guard was starting to tell on her nerves. It would be good to get away from the ship and relax for a few hours. Maybe it would help her put things into perspective. There was no point in continually blaming herself for not having trusted Liam when it wouldn't change what had happened. Their marriage was over. Period.

She was just about to go for breakfast when there was a knock on her cabin door. She hurried to answer it, smiling when she found Charlie Henshaw outside. 'Good morning, Charlie. How are you today?'

'Not too bad, thank you, miss.' He handed her a slip of paper. 'Message for you from the purser's office. I said I'd deliver it seeing as I was coming this way.'

'Oh, right. Thanks, Charlie.'

She went back inside and read the note. It was a message from the employment agency, informing her that a replacement nurse had been hired and would join the ship when it returned to Palma the following Saturday.

Sophie sank onto the bunk as it hit her that she had just seven more days left on board the ship. Even though she'd asked to be replaced, it still came as a shock to discover she would be leaving so soon.

She quickly skimmed through the rest of the message and sighed when she read the final paragraph, informing her that the cost of her flight home from Mallorca would be deducted from her salary because she'd broken the terms of her contract. Not only would she be out of a job in a week's time but she would be out of pocket as well, it seemed!

The realisation put rather a dampener on her plans for the day. She decided to skip breakfast in the dining-room because she wasn't in the mood to make conversation. She went to the LiteBite Café instead, ordered a large cup of coffee and took it back to the surgery.

Sitting down at the desk, she sipped the coffee while she tried to formulate some plans. As soon as she got back to England she would have to find another job. Obviously, she couldn't go back to the same agency when she was *persona non grata* there so she would have to contact a different one. Inevitably, that would mean time wasted while she went for interviews.

As for the kind of job she took, well, she certainly couldn't afford to be choosy. She'd spent the bulk of her savings on the clothes she'd bought for the trip and what little was left wouldn't last long if she had to pay rent and living costs. All things considered, it was rather a bleak outlook so it was hardly surprising that she was looking decidedly dejected when Liam arrived.

'What's up? You look as though you've lost a pound and found the proverbial penny.'

'Knowing my luck at the moment, I probably wouldn't even find the penny.' She sighed when he looked at her quizzically. 'The agency has found someone to replace me. They're going to fly her out to Palma next Saturday.'

'That was quick!'

Sophie shrugged, refusing to dwell on the fact that he'd sounded dismayed by the announcement. What difference did it make to Liam when she was leaving? 'They must have pulled out all the stops to find someone suitable.'

'So what will you do?' He frowned as he perched on the edge of the desk. 'You'll need a place to live for starters so can you go back to your old flat?'

'I doubt it. The landlord told me that he had someone interested in it so he's probably rented it out by now. Anyway, I've not decided where I'm going to live yet.'

'So you're not going back to Derbyshire, then?'

'I haven't made up my mind yet.'

She picked up a pen and started to doodle on the blotter because the thought of how uncertain the future was made her feel all panicky inside. She'd never been an impulsive sort of a person and wasn't used to having to make major decisions on the spur of the moment.

'But surely it would make more sense if you went back there? Starting off in a strange place, where you know nobody, won't be easy, Sophie, believe me.'

'I know that. I'm not a child, Liam, so, please, don't treat me like one!'

'I didn't mean to. I'm sorry. It's just that I'm worried about you.'

Her heart skipped a beat when she heard the genuine concern in his voice. She was sorely tempted to ask his advice, only it would be wrong to do that. Liam had his own life to think about and she couldn't expect him to solve her problems. She had to stand on her own two feet.

'And I didn't mean to snap,' she said quietly, staring fixedly at the patterns she'd made on the blotter when she felt her eyes fill with tears. The past few days had been a strain and now this coming on top was just too much to cope with.

'This is all my fault. If I hadn't been so damned set on sorting things out then you'd be carrying on exactly as you'd planned!'

Liam got up and angrily paced the floor. 'You'd have a good job on board this ship and another few months to decide what you really want to do, instead of being faced with all these problems.'

Sophie shook her head because it wasn't fair to let him think he was to blame for her predicament. 'You only did what you thought was right, Liam. If anyone's to blame then it's me.'

'You? How do you work that out?'

Her heart ached when she saw the frown on his face. It struck her then that if she'd been having a difficult time in the past few days, so, too, had Liam. Even though she'd decided never to mention the past again, she couldn't just leave things the way they were.

'Because I should have trusted you when you told me that you'd not had an affair,' she said truthfully.

'And I should have tried harder to convince you instead of letting my pride get in the way.' He sighed. 'Neither of us was thinking clearly because of what we'd been through and we failed to make any allowances for that.'

'We didn't. But at least we've cleared everything up now so that's one good thing that has come out of all this.'

'Ever the optimist, Sophie?' he said softly, and she flushed when she heard the warmth in his voice.

'Better than being a pessimist, even though it's a lot harder work.'

'What do you mean?'

'You try being upbeat when you're going to have to relinquish all this luxury!'

She summoned a smile but it was difficult to ignore the warmth that was seeping through her veins. 'There'll be no more cordon bleu meals served by waiters whose only aim in life is to tempt your jaded palate. No more stewards to clear up after you. I don't know how I'll cope with my usual humdrum existence now I've had a taste of the good life!'

'You'll manage.'

Liam's tone was warmer than ever and her temperature whooshed up another few degrees. Sophie tensed when he came over to the desk. It was difficult to hide how on edge she felt when he bent down so that his face was only inches away from hers. He studied her intently for several heart-melting seconds then slowly shook his head.

'Nope. I can't see any sign of them.'

'Any sign of what?' she demanded sharply, because her heart was in serious danger of turning to mush.

'Your halo and wings, of course.' He chuckled when she looked at him blankly. 'Only a real, bona fide angel could remain so positive in the face of such adversity. It's just working out where you've hidden your angel accoutrements that puzzles me.'

'Idiot!' she retorted, her tension swept away by a sudden rush of laughter.

'That's better.' He touched the tiny mole at the corner of her mouth with the tip of one long finger. 'There's nothing better than an angel with a smile on her lips.'

Sophie's laughter abruptly faded when she saw the expression in his eyes. Maybe it was crazy to let herself get carried away by what it seemed to be telling her, but she couldn't help it. Liam was looking at her as though she was the most special person in the whole world, and it was an amazing feeling.

She wasn't sure what might have happened if there hadn't been a knock on the door at that moment. Liam straightened abruptly but she could hear the roughness in his voice, a betraying sign that he'd been as deeply affected by that look they'd shared as she had been.

'Sounds as though our first patient has arrived. Would you mind taking down the details while I get ready?'

'Of course.'

Sophie got up from her desk as he went into the consulting room. She went to the door but paused to take a deep breath before she opened it. She wanted to be sure that none of the turmoil she felt showed on her face, although it was hopeless trying to pretend that nothing had happened. Liam had looked at her just now as though she still meant something to him, but surely that couldn't be true?

'Paul said I was making a lot of fuss about nothing but I just wanted to check, Dr Kennedy.'

'And you were right to do so, Mrs Rogers.' Liam smiled reassuringly at the anxious young woman who was cradling a baby in her arms. The little girl was just three months old and had been suffering from sickness and diarrhoea during the night. Although she didn't appear to be seriously ill, he didn't intend to take any chances.

'Young babies like Lucy soon become dehydrated so it's essential to seek medical advice whenever something like this happens. I'm going to prescribe an electrolyte mixture, which will replace the water and salts she's lost. Don't give her any milk for the next twenty-four hours then, if the symptoms have cleared up, you can gradually re-introduce it.'

He jotted some notes on a piece of paper and handed it to Angela Rogers. 'The first feed should consist of one part milk to three of water, the second of equal parts milk and water, the third three parts milk to one of water and the fourth feed can be undiluted milk. Is that clear?'

'I think so.' Angela frowned as she read through the instructions. She seemed very tense and anxious, and his tone softened.

'Don't worry too much about it now. Bring Lucy back to see me in the morning and I'll run through it all again. The main thing to concentrate on at the moment is making sure she doesn't become dehydrated. However, I'm sure she's going to be fine.'

'Thank you, Doctor. I expect you think it's silly but I tend to panic when she seems a bit off-colour.' Tears welled into the young mother's eyes as she looked at the child. 'I lost a baby before I had Lucy, you see. She was stillborn and I'm so scared something is going to happen to Lucy as well…'

She bit her lip. Liam reached across the desk and patted her hand. He understood only too well what she must be going through and his heart ached for her.

'Lucy will be fine. This is just one of those minor setbacks that happen to many babies,' he said huskily, because his own anguish at losing Zoë made the young mother's story all the more poignant. 'By tomorrow morning, she will be much better. You'll see. But make sure you bring her back so I can check her over and run through the feeding regime again.'

'You're very kind.' Angela wiped her eyes with a tissue. 'It gets Paul down because I keep worrying all the time that something is going to happen to her. That's why he wanted us to come on this cruise. He thought it would be good for us to get away and have a complete change of scene.'

'I'm sure it will help, although you're bound to worry. It's only natural in the circumstances.' He frowned. 'Were you planning on going ashore today? To be honest, Mrs Rogers, I don't think it would be wise to take Lucy out in this heat.'

'We were going to do some sightseeing but not any more,' she said firmly. 'I'm going to stay on board the ship and if Paul still wants to go then that's up to him.'

'I think it would be best,' Liam agreed, inwardly sighing because it was obvious the trip was creating more problems for the young couple than it was resolving.

He saw Angela out, thinking how sad it was that people found it so difficult to talk to each other. Loving someone didn't always mean you were able to communicate your feelings to them. Sometimes it was because you were afraid of hurting them, as had been the case with him and Sophie.

His heart filled with a mixture of emotions as he glanced at her. He'd desperately wanted to protect her from the pain of their child's death but he'd not allowed for the fact that he'd been too stricken by grief himself to help her. It was a mistake he would have to live with for the rest of his life.

There were no more patients to see so Liam wrote up the case notes then went back to the office and dropped the file in the tray on Sophie's desk. 'Looks as though that's it for today. Folk are obviously more interested in going ashore than being ill.'

'I don't blame them.' She picked up the file and quickly

entered the details into the computer. 'I intend to go
ashore once I've finished this.'

'Of course, it's your day off, isn't it?' He grinned.
'What are you planning on doing? Hitting the shops in
Valletta?'

'No, I thought something a bit more educational today.'
She printed out a copy of the notes for the accounting
department and gave it to him to sign. 'I'm going to
M'dina which, according to my guidebook, was Malta's
original capital city.'

'Oh, pardon me!' He scrawled his signature in the space
at the bottom and passed the sheet back to her. 'I'd forgotten what a culture vulture you are.'

'Culture vulture?' She burst out laughing and he felt
his heart lift because it had been a long time since he'd
heard such unaffected pleasure in her voice. 'I hope that
wasn't a dig at me?'

'Of course not!' he denied, grinning at her. 'Just because you once told me that if you saw another museum
you'd scream doesn't mean that I think you are a shallow
person...'

'Any *normal* person would have been fed up if they'd
been dragged round every single museum in London! I
mean, there's only so much culture the average person
can absorb in one day.'

'I know. I know.' He held up his hands. 'And I'm sorry,
both for the gibe and the fact that I dragged you round
all those exhibitions. I just couldn't bring myself to tell
you that I was broke and couldn't afford to take you
somewhere more glamorous. I was still at the desperately-
wanting-to-impress-you stage, you see.'

'Thank heavens it wore off,' she retorted. 'If I'd had to
ooh and ah over another piece of broken pottery, I'd have

gone barking mad. I was starting to have serious doubts as to whether I'd made a mistake by going out with you!'

'Maybe you did,' he said flatly, because it hurt to imagine how different her life might have been if she'd met and married someone else. She might have had a home and a family by this stage, all the things she'd always dreamed of having. He couldn't help feeling guilty because of the way things had turned out for them.

'I disagree. I don't regret meeting you, Liam. I never have. The only thing I regret is how badly it all ended. Still, there's no point dwelling on that now, is there? It's all in the past and we have to concentrate on the future.'

She stood up. 'And talking about the future, I'd better take this to the office before I go ashore.'

'Yes. Of course,' he replied hollowly.

He sat down at the desk after she left because his legs suddenly felt too weak to support him. He'd always believed that Sophie had regretted falling in love with him, but it wasn't true. What she regretted was the way her love for him had ended.

His heart spasmed with pain because the thought that she no longer loved him was just so hard to bear.

The sun was beating down on the walled city of M'dina, raising the temperature to a level that soon had Sophie wilting. She'd slathered sunscreen all over her arms and legs and worn a hat to shade her face, but she simply wasn't used to such temperatures. After just an hour spent exploring, she was ready to leave, but the thought of returning to the ship was more than she could bear. She needed a bit more time on her own after the conversation she'd had with Liam that morning.

Pain speared through her and she sighed. Talking about how much she'd loved Liam had brought back all the heartache, but there was no point thinking about it. She'd come ashore with the express intention of getting away from her problems so she would take a break then visit the cathedral in Pjazza San Pawl. According to her guide-book, there was a magnificent fresco of the shipwreck of St Paul in the apse which she wanted to see.

She spotted a sign directing her to a tearoom when she reached the end of the street. She went inside and ordered a bottle of mineral water and a sandwich then went to find herself a seat on the terrace. All the tables in the shade were taken and she was just turning to go back inside when she spotted Randolph Walters waving to her.

'Looks like you two have had the same idea as me,' she said as she went over to their table.

'Gloria was starting to feel a little uncomfortable from all this heat so we thought we'd have a rest,' Randolph explained, getting up to courteously pull out a chair for Sophie to sit down.

'It really is scorchingly hot today,' she agreed. She glanced at Gloria and frowned when she saw how pale the older woman looked. Beads of perspiration were standing out on Gloria's upper lip and forehead, even though it was relatively cool in this part of the terrace.

'Are you feeling all right, Gloria?' she asked in con-cern.

'Oh, I'll be fine once I've had chance to cool down,' the woman assured her.

Sophie wasn't convinced but she decided not to press the point. The waiter arrived with her order so she cut into her sandwich while Randolph told her about all the places they'd visited since they'd left the ship. They seemed to have crammed an awful lot into a short space of time, especially bearing in mind how hot it was that day. Sophie was just thinking it was little wonder Gloria looked worn out when she heard the older woman gasp as she clutched her chest.

'What's wrong, Gloria? Are you in pain?'

'Yes… Oh, it really hurts!'

Sophie got up and hurried around the table. 'Where is the pain? Just in the centre of your chest?'

'It started off in my chest but now it's in my throat and in my jaw as well…' Gloria broke off and groaned.

It was obvious the pain was getting worse so Sophie turned to Randolph, who was staring at his wife in horror. 'I think we need an ambulance, Randolph. Can you ask one of the waiters to phone—?'

'No. No ambulance… Just need my bag.'

Sophie looked round when Gloria clutched her arm. 'You have medication with you?'

'A spray the doctor gave me…'

Sophie didn't waste any more time as she grabbed Gloria's bag and emptied its contents onto the table. She quickly found the spray of glyceryl trinitrate, a drug which was frequently prescribed for angina. Removing the top, she turned back to Gloria.

'Open your mouth for me. You'll soon feel better.' She quickly sprayed the medication into the woman's mouth and waited for it to take effect. She smiled when she saw the dawning relief on Gloria's face. 'Better now?'

'Oh, yes, much. The pain's easing off now.'

'I don't understand what's going on. Where did you get that, Gloria, and why do you need it?'

Sophie frowned when she heard the bewilderment in Randolph's voice. If she wasn't mistaken, his wife's illness had come as a complete surprise to him.

'Dr Maguire prescribed it, honey. I've been having some pains in my chest and he told me that they were caused by angina,' Gloria explained rather sheepishly. 'He said that if I had an attack then the spray would help, and it has.'

'Angina!' Randolph ran a trembling hand over his face. 'I just don't understand why you never told me.'

'Because I didn't want to worry you.' Gloria patted his hand and Sophie felt a lump come to her throat when she saw the loving look the older woman gave her husband.

'I knew how much you were looking forward to this trip, honey. I also knew that if you found out I'd been feeling ill, you'd have cancelled it.' Gloria sighed. 'I decided not to tell you until we got back home. Dr Maguire assured me I'd be fine if I took the tablets he prescribed for me, and made sure I had the spray with me, and he was right. I feel a whole lot better now!'

Randolph shook his head. 'I still can't believe you kept it a secret from me.' He turned to Sophie and she could see the fear in his eyes. 'Is it correct what Gloria says? Will she be all right?'

'If your doctor says so then I'm sure it must be true,' she said carefully, because it would be wrong to give an opinion she wasn't qualified to make. 'A lot of people live with angina for many years and they learn how to deal with it. I imagine the heat was what triggered Gloria's attack today.'

'The heat?' Randolph repeated dubiously.

'Yes. Extremes of temperature are well known for triggering angina attacks,' she explained patiently. 'The pain is caused by insufficient oxygen getting to the heart muscle, usually because the arteries have narrowed. Changes in temperature and excessive exercise can both bring on attacks.'

'But will it get worse and will Gloria have more of these attacks?' Randolph demanded.

'I'm really not qualified to say.' Sophie smiled reassuringly. 'The fact that the medication was so effective today is a good sign, but I'd advise you to have a word with Dr Kennedy when you get back to the ship. He'll be able to tell you more about your wife's condition and what you can expect to happen.'

'I'll do that.' Randolph held up his hand when Gloria started to tell him it wasn't necessary. 'Maybe it isn't but I'd like to hear that for myself. You are far too precious to me to take any chances with your health.'

'Oh, Randolph, honey, I'm so sorry!'

Sophie excused herself and went to the rest room to give the couple a few minutes on their own. She washed her hands at the tiny basin, sighing when she caught sight of herself in the mirror on the wall. Once upon a time she'd envisaged herself and Liam being like the other couple—growing old together and coping with whatever problems occurred—only it hadn't worked out that way.

Now Liam would spend his life with another woman, and as for her…well, she wasn't sure what would happen to her. She definitely couldn't imagine herself getting married again. If it hadn't worked out with Liam then what chance was there of her finding happiness with someone else? She certainly couldn't love anyone as much as she loved Liam.

Her heart jolted when it struck her that she'd used the present tense and not the past. A small mental hiccup, perhaps, or something more revealing?

The answer should have been obvious but for some reason she found herself wavering. She couldn't put her hand on her heart and swear that what she felt for Liam was all in the past.

CHAPTER NINE

LIAM was on his way to his cabin when he spotted Sophie getting out of a taxi. Randolph and Gloria Walters were with her and he frowned when he saw her helping Gloria up the gangplank. It was obvious that something was wrong so he hurried to meet them.

'What's happened?' he asked, trying to control the surge his heart gave when he saw what Sophie was wearing.

She'd changed out of her uniform for the trip ashore into a short-sleeved lemon shirt and a cotton skirt in shades of citrus and lime. She'd had the good sense to wear a hat—a creamy woven straw with a wide brim that shaded her face and a jaunty yellow ribbon around the crown. She looked so young and lovely that it was an effort not to stare. However, Liam was very much aware that she wouldn't appreciate his interest after what she'd said that morning.

'Gloria wasn't feeling well so we decided it would be best if she came back to the ship,' she explained.

'I see.'

He could tell there was more to the tale but decided it would be best to get Gloria to her cabin before he asked any more questions. He took over from Sophie, slipping a supporting arm around the elderly woman's waist as they made their way to the Walterses' cabin.

'Let's get you on the bed, Mrs Walters.' He helped her to the bunk then moved aside while Sophie packed pillows behind her back. Randolph had sunk down onto a chair and Liam could tell how shaken the old man appeared to be.

'Would you mind ringing the steward and ask him to bring a pot of tea?' he quietly instructed Sophie.

'Of course.'

She went to the phone while Liam drew up a chair beside the bunk. He smiled at Gloria. 'So what's been going on? Was it the heat that made you feel ill?'

'I have angina,' Gloria admitted. 'Sophie said it was probably the heat which triggered the attack today, though.'

'It could have done, especially if you've been doing a lot of walking around.' Liam checked her pulse. 'That seems fine at the moment but I'd like to check you over just to be on the safe side. What medication are you taking? I assume you do have some with you?'

'Yes. I have tablets which my doctor prescribed.' Gloria reached for the vanity case on her bedside table and handed him a blister-pack of pills.

'Glyceryl trinitrate,' he said, reading the label. 'That's fine. It's one of the oldest drugs still in use and highly effective in many cases of angina. Do you have a spray as well?'

'Yes. I carry it with me all the time.'

'Good.' He handed the packet back to Gloria then looked round when Sophie appeared at his side.

'There's a tray of tea on its way.' She glanced towards the door, silently indicating that she would like a word with him in private.

'Excellent. I'll just fetch my bag while we're waiting for it to arrive.'

Liam got up and followed her to the door. 'I won't be long,' he assured the elderly couple before he left the cabin. Sophie was waiting in the corridor for him and he turned to her as soon as he'd shut the door.

'So what's been going on?'

'It turns out that Gloria hadn't told Randolph that she has angina. She only told him today because she had an attack while they were sightseeing in M'dina.' She sounded worried. 'I'm not sure if she's making light of how bad it really is to stop him worrying.'

'Tricky situation. Obviously we have to respect her wishes but we need to have a proper idea what we might be dealing with.'

'Exactly!' She smiled in relief and he realised just how concerned she'd been.

'Gloria will be fine,' he assured her, thinking how typical it was of her to worry like that. Sophie had always invested far more of herself than could be expected in her work. She really cared about people and wanted what was best for them. It was yet another thing he'd always loved about her.

'I'll give her a thorough examination so I can get a better idea about the situation.' He briskly rid himself of that thought because it wouldn't help to keep listing all Sophie's good points. 'Maybe she'll tell me more if Randolph isn't there. Is there any way you could get him out of the way for a while?'

'I could try, but I'm not sure it will work.' She shrugged when he looked at her quizzically. 'He's extremely upset because Gloria didn't tell him about her illness. I doubt he'll be prepared to leave her on her own, to be honest.'

'Then let's hope she decides to come clean and tell us both the truth. It would be a lot easier at the end of the day. Trying to protect someone's feelings might be fine in principle but it can lead to a lot of problems.'

He could tell immediately that she'd guessed he'd been thinking about the problems they'd encountered. He turned away because there was no point going over it all again. 'I'll fetch my bag and we'll go from there.'

He went to the surgery and collected his bag. By the time he got back to the Walterses' cabin the tea had arrived. He smiled when he saw everyone decorously sipping the reviving liquid.

'There's nothing like a cup of tea to steady your nerves.'

'A shot of bourbon would be even better,' Randolph returned.

'Now, honey, you know very well that you aren't allowed to drink alcohol because of your blood pressure,' Gloria scolded.

'That's as may be but at least you know what's wrong with me whereas I had no idea that you'd been ill.'

'There's no point getting upset about what's happened,' Liam cut in quickly when he saw how agitated Randolph looked. 'Our main concern at the moment is to make sure that Gloria will be fine for the remainder of the trip.'

'I think we should forget about the holiday and go straight back home.' Randolph's tone was firm now. 'I don't intend to take any chances on this happening again.'

'Just because your wife suffered an attack today, it doesn't mean she will have another one,' Liam assured him. 'Obviously, I need to give her a thorough examination, and it would help if I could have a word with her doctor, but so long as Gloria keeps taking her medication then she should be fine.'

'Please, don't say that we have to go home, honey,' Gloria pleaded. 'You know how much we've been looking forward to this trip.'

'Well, we'll see,' Randolph conceded when he saw her

disappointment. 'If Dr Kennedy thinks you're fit enough to continue, I'll be guided by him. But you're to take things easy from now on, d'you hear me?'

'Oh, yes. Anything you say, Randolph.'

Liam breathed a sigh of relief that a compromise had been reached. He checked Gloria's blood pressure, pulse and respiratory rates and also took down the name and telephone number of her doctor back home in Georgia so he could contact him.

'Everything appears to be fine at the moment, although I suggest that Gloria rests for the remainder of the day.' He rolled up his stethoscope and popped it in his case. 'I honestly can't see any reason why you should cut short your holiday but you can make up your mind what you intend to do after I've spoken to your doctor. We're due at Naples in the morning so if you do decide to leave the ship then the hospitality team will be able to arrange flights home for you.'

'Thank you, Dr Kennedy.' Randolph stood up and shook hands. 'I appreciate your advice.' He turned to Sophie and smiled warmly. 'And thank you, my dear. I don't know what I'd have done if you hadn't been there when Gloria had that attack.'

'I'm pleased I was able to help.' She laughed. 'I told you that you'd feel better after you'd spoken to Dr Kennedy, didn't I?'

Liam's heart swelled. He couldn't help being touched by her confidence in him. He bid the Walterses goodbye and left their cabin. Sophie followed him out and he heard her sigh as they made their way towards the hospital bay.

'Eventful day?' he asked, smiling at her.

'You could say that.' She returned his smile and he felt his heart lift when he saw the laughter in her beautiful blue eyes. 'Although I didn't get much time for sightseeing. I never even made it to the cathedral because I was too concerned about getting Gloria back to the ship.'

'So you're suffering from an *under*dose of culture today, are you?' he teased, referring back to their earlier conversation.

'You could say that!' She chuckled. 'You'll never let me live that down, will you?'

'Nope. It's good to score the odd point.'

'Horrible man!' she retorted, pulling a face at him.

'I'm not being horrible.' He laughed as they walked down the steps together. 'I'm just trying to keep your feet on the ground by pointing out that you do have the odd flaw in your character.'

'Thanks very much.' She elbowed the swing doors open. 'If you're not careful, I'll start looking for flaws in your character, too.'

'I've never claimed to be perfect,' he replied loftily, earning himself a speaking look.

'Mmm, I don't think I'll answer that. It might be safer to let it pass.' She waited while he unlocked the surgery door. 'Anyway, back to Gloria. Are you going to get in touch with her doctor and see what he says?'

'Yes. I'd like a word with him even though I honestly don't believe there's any reason to panic about what happened today.'

Liam put his case on the desk and turned to her. She was standing in the doorway and he felt heat pool in the pit of his stomach when he saw how the light shining along the corridor had turned her skirt semi-transparent. He could see her shapely thighs outlined beneath the fine cotton material and had to look away when his body immediately reacted to the sight.

'So long as she doesn't try doing too much, she should be fine,' he said thickly.

'That's what I told Randolph. Obviously it was a shock for him to discover that Gloria has angina, but I'm hoping he won't decide to cut short their holiday. It would be such a shame, wouldn't it?'

'It would.'

Liam decided it was time he put an end to the torture. The temptation to look at Sophie again was unbearable but he refused to put himself under that kind of stress. There was no point wishing he could take her in his arms and make love to her because he didn't have the right to do that.

His breath caught when he realised in which direction his thoughts had led him. Making love to Sophie wasn't an option for any number of reasons, the main one being that he was supposed to be marrying Julia in a few months' time. It was just proving incredibly difficult to keep sight of that fact.

He checked his watch, deeming it safer to focus on work because once he started thinking about his private life, everything fell apart. 'I'd better get myself to the purser's office and phone Dr Maguire. It's just before eight a.m. in Georgia and I might be able to catch him before he sees any patients.'

'Good idea. Let me know what he says, Liam, won't you?' She groaned as she used her hat to fan herself. 'I am absolutely boiling! What I need is a nice cool dip in the pool so that's where I'll be if you want me.'

'Fine.' Liam held his smile until she'd left but he knew there was no way he was going to seek her out. The thought of Sophie in a swimsuit was more temptation than any red-blooded male could be expected to withstand!

He locked the surgery and went to the purser's office to phone the Walterses' doctor. The man couldn't have been more helpful when Liam explained who he was and what had happened. He thanked Dr Maguire and hung up, wondering if he should have a word with the elderly couple and tell them that Dr Maguire had given them his blessing to continue their holiday. In the end, however, he decided to wait until the morning because he didn't want it to appear as though he was pushing them into making a decision. There was still almost an hour left before he needed to get ready for dinner so he went to the LiteBite Café and ordered himself a large glass of chilled fruit juice.

He sat down at a table by the window to drink it, hoping it would help to clear his mind if he sat quietly for a while. Although he was no longer surprised by his response to Sophie, it did worry him. He'd taken this job, confident that he'd be able to get on with his life once he'd sorted out their past mistakes, but it wasn't working out that way. The more time he spent with Sophie, the harder it was to imagine a future without her.

Liam sighed as he put the glass on the table. He could beat about the bush for ever but there was really only one course open to him in the circumstances: he would have to tell Julia that he couldn't marry her. Although he hated the thought of letting her down, he knew it was the right thing to do. He couldn't go ahead with the wedding when Sophie still had this much of a hold over him.

His hand shook just a little as he picked up the glass because there was no way he could avoid the truth. Although their marriage might be over, the ties that bound him to Sophie were impossible to break.

The weather started to change almost as soon as they left Malta. Huge black clouds began to gather along the horizon and a strong wind sprang up. The sea became increasingly rough so that several times Sophie had to grab hold of the furniture while she was getting ready for dinner. She wasn't surprised when Charlie Henshaw knocked on her cabin door and warned her they were expecting a storm to break later that evening.

She went to the dining-room, wondering how the change in the weather would affect the passengers. Although she was feeling fine, she suspected that a lot of people would be affected by the sudden increase in motion. Liam obviously shared her concerns because he was waiting outside the dining-room for her and drew her to one side.

'I'm going to open the surgery after dinner. Yuri is going to make an announcement to that effect over the loudspeaker system. A lot of people will probably start feeling ill pretty soon so I'll be available to hand out sea-sickness tablets to those who need them.'

'Good idea.' She clutched hold of his arm when the ship suddenly rolled to the side. 'Oops, sorry!'

'That's OK. Anyway, you don't need to be there. I know it's your day off, Sophie, and I don't expect you to work. I just wanted to let you know what was happening.'

'Of course I'll be there,' she protested. 'It's my job to look after the passengers, isn't it?'

'Well, if you're sure you don't mind, it would be a help if there were two of us.'

He smiled at her and Sophie had to make a determined effort to control the little flutter her heart gave. It was casual dress that evening and she couldn't help thinking how handsome he looked in the crisp white shirt and navy trousers. Liam had always possessed an innate elegance which stemmed partly from his height and partly from the aura of confidence he exuded. She'd never been more aware of it than she was that night, strangely enough.

'Some folk might not be able to make it to the surgery

so I may need to visit them in their cabins,' he explained. 'I can leave you to hold the fort in my absence, if you don't mind.'

'That's fine by me,' she agreed, willing the nervous fluttering to abate. 'With a bit of luck the storm will pass over soon and everything will be back to normal.'

'Let's hope you're right,' he observed wryly as the ship heaved again, making the glasses on the dining-room tables rattle noisily. 'Otherwise we could be in for a busy night.'

The words turned out to be prophetic. As soon as they finished dinner they went back to the hospital and opened up the surgery. They had a steady stream of visitors for the rest of the evening so that by the time ten o'clock arrived, Sophie had logged up over fifty people who'd required sea-sickness tablets and there were half a dozen more in the waiting room.

'If it carries on like this, we're going to run out,' she said, anxiously checking the drugs cupboard.

'Mike Soames told me they keep extra supplies in the hold so we should be fine,' Liam assured her. He grimaced when the ship bucked as it hit a particularly large wave. 'The storm seems to be getting worse. Do you have any idea how long it will take before we clear it?'

'No, but surely it can't last much longer.' She couldn't quite keep the concern out of her voice and she saw him frown.

'You're not scared, are you? The *Esmeralda* is one of the most modern cruise ships around. It has every sort of safety feature imaginable.'

'So did the *Titanic* and look what happened to that,' she retorted.

He laughed. 'I doubt we'll run into any icebergs in the middle of the Mediterranean, sweetheart.'

Sophie's heart skipped a beat when she heard the endearment. She knew it was foolish to set any store by it but she couldn't help herself. She returned his smile, hoping he couldn't tell how much it had affected her to hear him speak to her in that warmly caring tone.

'I'll take your word for that. And now I'd better send in the next poor soul.'

'You do that.'

He was all business once more and she sighed as she went to summon the next patient. Liam was finding it as difficult as she was to separate the past from the present, but it didn't mean he still loved her, and it hurt to realise that.

It was almost eleven before they finally locked up and by that time Sophie was exhausted. The constant motion of the ship, combined with the tension which had plagued her all day, had given her a headache. Liam looked at her in concern as he slipped the surgery keys into his pocket.

'You don't look so good. Do you feel sick?'

'No, I've got a headache. I kept meaning to take some aspirin but I never seemed to get the chance because we were so busy.'

'We've run out of aspirin, I'm afraid. I've just put in a requisition for some more, in fact, but it will be morning before they fetch up the supplies. I've got some paracetamol tablets in my cabin, though, if they would help,' he offered immediately.

'Thanks,' she replied gratefully. 'I never thought to pack anything like that because I rarely ever get a headache.'

'Come along, then. Let me get them for you.'

He led the way to his cabin and opened the door. Sophie hesitated but it seemed ridiculous to stand outside like a nervous schoolgirl. She sat on the bunk while Liam went to the bathroom for the tablets. He returned a few moments later and went straight to the tiny fridge and took out a bottle of mineral water. Breaking the seal on the cap, he half filled a glass and gave it to her.

'Here you go.'

'Thanks.' Sophie popped the tablets into her mouth and washed them down with some of the water.

'It will take a while for them to work, I'm afraid. Just how bad is your headache?'

'Pretty grim,' she admitted. She rolled her shoulders to try and relieve the pressure that had built up at the base of her skull.

'Turn round.' Before she could protest, Liam placed his hands on her shoulders and turned her so that her back was towards him.

'What are you doing?' she demanded in alarm when she felt his fingers glide over the nape of her neck.

'I'm just going to give you a massage. You're all tensed up, Sophie, and that's making your headache worse.'

'Oh, but there's no need. Really!' She tried to shrug off his hands but he didn't release her.

'Relax. You're quite safe. I know what I'm doing.'

His fingers moved from her nape to her hairline and gently began massaging the base of her skull. Sophie closed her eyes as a shiver ran through her. The warm touch of his hands felt so wonderful but she was afraid of what might happen if she relaxed.

'Stop tensing up. You're just making matters worse.' He used his thumbs to gently knead the knotted muscles in her neck and a reluctant sigh escaped her.

'That's better,' he said softly, without breaking the rhythm. 'Just close your eyes and let yourself go limp. I'm not going to hurt you. I promise.'

Sophie closed her eyes purely and simply because she

couldn't resist. She exhaled softly when she felt Liam's fingers move further up her skull and begin to massage it in a soothing motion that almost had her purring with pleasure.

'Where did you learn to give massages?' she murmured, because it seemed wiser to keep at least some of her wits about her.

'While I was working at a hospice for the terminally ill in India.'

His tone was just as quiet as hers had been yet she felt a ripple of shock run through her. 'I didn't know you'd worked in India as well!'

'I was only there for a couple of months before I went to Africa. It was my first posting for the aid agency, a sort of test to see how I coped with both the work and the conditions.'

He carried on massaging her skull while he spoke, his fingers moving in gentle circular motions now. 'The staff at the hospice had very little in the way of modern medicines to give their patients so they had to rely on traditional remedies to relieve pain. Massage can be a highly effective means of reducing pain because it creates counter-irritation in the nerve endings in the skin. The staff at the clinic were all experts at it and I learned a lot from them.'

'There's so many things you've done in the past couple of years that I didn't know about,' she admitted sadly.

'There's no way you could have known, Sophie.' His hands stilled. 'We went our separate ways after the divorce, didn't we? I had no way of knowing what you were doing, for that matter.'

'That's easy. I stayed exactly where I was, doing the same job.' She sighed. 'No wonder we split up when it's obvious we both wanted such very different things out of life.'

'That's not true.' His tone was fierce all of a sudden and she jumped.

'No?' She knew she should let it drop but something drove her on. For some reason it seemed important that she find out how he really felt about their marriage.

'No,' he repeated, but more quietly this time. 'All right, so circumstances might have dictated that I made a career change, but I was happy with the life we had. I certainly never felt that I'd missed out in any way.'

'And yet if you hadn't gone overseas then you would never have met Julia,' she pointed out reasonably.

'No. I don't expect I would.'

Sophie frowned when she heard the sombre note in his voice. Was he thinking how empty his life might have been if he hadn't met Julia, perhaps? It seemed the most logical explanation yet she wasn't convinced it was the real one. It was a relief when he changed the subject because it would be far too easy to start looking for a deeper meaning that probably didn't exist. She had to remember that Liam was happy with the new life he had made for himself.

'So how does your head feel now? Any better?'

'Much.' Sophie summoned a smile but it hurt to be reminded that Liam had someone else to share his dreams now. He and Julia would probably have children one day and the thought was so painful that she couldn't bear it.

She hurriedly stood up, knowing that she had to leave before she made a fool of herself. It would be wrong to begrudge him the family he'd always dreamed of having, but it just seemed to bring it home to her how much she had lost.

'I'd better go. It's late and we could be busy again in the morning if this bad weather continues.'

'Hopefully, the sea will be a bit calmer when we reach the Italian coast.' He caught hold of her arm when she went to hurry past him and she could see the concern in his eyes. 'Are you sure you're all right, Sophie? You still don't look too good.'

'I'm fine. Or I shall be after a good night's sleep.' Her smile was a shade too bright but it was the best she could manage. She was only human and it hurt to know that another woman was going to fulfill his dreams.

He didn't try to stop her again when she moved away. She hurried to the door and paused to glance back. Liam was still sitting on the bunk and there was the strangest expression on his face, a kind of yearning that immediately touched her heart. He looked so sad and lonely that she was tempted to go back and ask him what was wrong, only it would be a mistake to do that. He didn't need her comfort or her help when he had Julia!

Tears filled her eyes and she quickly turned away before he saw them. 'I'll see you in the morning,' she murmured as she let herself out.

'Goodnight, Sophie.'

The words floated after her as she crossed the passage and let herself into her own cabin. She closed the door then went to the porthole and stood there, watching the black swell of the waves pounding against the ship. What was that saying about time and tide waiting for no man? It was true, too, because she couldn't turn back time any more than she could turn back those waves, but it didn't stop her wishing that she could. If she could relive the past few years, she would do things differently. She would listen to Liam and believe him when he told her he wasn't having an affair. She would trust him because she loved him and because she knew in her heart that he loved her as well.

It was all so simple that she couldn't understand how she'd lost sight of the truth two years ago. Maybe it had been her grief over Zoë's death but that was no excuse. She should have known in her heart that Liam would never have betrayed her! Now it was too late to put matters right and far too late to wish they could try again because he loved someone else.

CHAPTER TEN

THE weather had improved considerably by the time they reached Naples the following morning. It was still very hot but the sea was much calmer. Nevertheless, there were a number of empty places at breakfast, a sure sign that some passengers were still suffering the after-effects of the storm.

Liam took his place at the table, wondering where Sophie had got to. She was normally in her seat by the time he arrived but there was no sign of her that morning. Gloria and Randolph were also missing so he made a note to visit them in their cabin as soon as he'd finished breakfast.

Sophie still hadn't appeared by the time Liam left the dining-room and he was torn between a desire to check if she was all right and a need to tell the Walterses what their doctor had said the previous day. In the end, duty won because if the Walterses did decide to leave the ship that day then he would have to liaise with the hospitality team so they could make the necessary arrangements.

He went straight to their cabin and knocked on the door. Randolph opened it and he laughed when he saw him. 'Good morning, Dr Kennedy. This is a day for visitors, it seems. Come along in and join the party.'

Liam went into the cabin and felt his heart lift when he discovered Sophie was there. 'So this is where you've got to. I wondered if you'd succumbed to the dreaded sea-sickness.'

'Not so far, I'm pleased to say.' She gave him a tight

little smile as she stood up. 'I'll leave you to have a word with Dr Kennedy, Gloria. I'm so glad the storm didn't affect you too badly last night.'

'Thank you, honey. We sure do appreciate you dropping by to see how we are.' Gloria turned to Liam and smiled. 'You are a very lucky man to have such a lovely young woman working with you, Dr Kennedy. I hope you appreciate her.'

'I do,' Liam replied, hoping Sophie hadn't heard the husky note in his voice. Gloria's comment had touched a chord because he did appreciate her, far too much, in fact.

He sat down to explain to the Walterses what their doctor had said after Sophie left. Randolph was understandably concerned about his wife so it took some time to answer his questions. Liam was glad, however, because it gave him less time to worry about his own problems as he concentrated on convincing Randolph that Gloria was well enough to continue the holiday. He obviously succeeded because in the end Randolph decided they would stay on the ship, much to Gloria's delight.

Liam went straight to the surgery after leaving the Walterses' cabin and discovered there was a crowd in the waiting room again. He didn't have a chance to tell Sophie about the elderly couple's decision because people were eager to be seen before they went ashore. A trip to Pompeii was the highlight of that day's visit to port and a lot of people had booked to go on it.

Liam prescribed antiemetics for all those who required them. More storms were forecast for the coming week and nobody wanted to take the chance of being caught out. It was almost ten before the last patient had been seen and he grimaced as he handed the paperwork to Sophie.

'There's quite a stack today, I'm afraid. What's the bet

that we won't have another night like the last one now everyone is prepared for the worst?'

'Probably not.' She took the files from him. 'Are you going ashore today? It's your day off, isn't it?'

'That's right.'

'So what are your plans? Are you going on the trip to Pompeii?' she queried, sorting the files into order so she could enter the details into the computer. Although there was no charge levied for sea-sickness medication, a record needed to be kept of everyone who was seen in the surgery each day.

'No, I think I'll give it a miss. There's something I need to do,' he replied abstractedly, wondering if he should put in another requisition for antiemetics. They'd already made inroads into the supplies that had been sent up that morning and he didn't want to take the chance of them running out.

'Oh?'

Liam bit back a sigh when he heard the curiosity in her voice. He didn't want to be drawn into saying too much but he could hardly refuse to tell her why he was going ashore.

'I need to get in touch with Julia,' he explained. 'Unfortunately, there's no telephone where she's working so I'll have to contact the aid agency's headquarters in the region and ask them to get a message to her. They have a satellite phone in their office so she can call me on that when it's convenient.'

'Sounds very complicated. Still, I'm sure you must be looking forward to hearing from her. Let's hope it won't be too long before she gets in touch.'

She gave him a quick smile then turned her attention back to her work. Liam hesitated, wondering if he should have explained why he was so eager to speak to Julia. He hated to think he'd misled Sophie in any way but it wouldn't be fair to tell her that he'd decided to call off the wedding before he told Julia, would it?

He made the call as soon as he reached shore and was surprised when he discovered that Julia was on leave. He couldn't recall her mentioning that she was taking any leave before her contract expired but maybe a problem had cropped up at home. Although she never spoke about her family, she occasionally received mail from England so he'd always assumed that she had relatives there. He sighed because it brought it home to him again how little he really knew about her.

The person at the agency was unable to give him a number where he could reach her so Liam had to be content with leaving a message, asking her to get in touch. However, as he hung up he couldn't help wishing that Julia hadn't chosen this particular time to disappear. Now that he'd made up his mind what he was going to do, he was impatient to get everything sorted out so he could make fresh plans…

His heart sank when he realised how stupid it was to hope that Sophie would play any part in those plans. Once she left the ship, that would be the end of the matter. Quite frankly, he didn't know how he was going to cope. He could tell himself a thousand times that they'd had their chance at happiness but it didn't stop him wishing they could try again.

The days flew past, far too fast so far as Sophie was concerned. Each new day that dawned brought her one day closer to when she would be leaving the ship. She tried to tell herself that it was the worry about having to find another job and somewhere to live that was making her feel so downhearted, but she knew it wasn't the real explanation. It was the thought of leaving Liam that was so hard to deal with.

There was a full day's sailing scheduled for the Thursday. As she got dressed, Sophie found herself wondering if they would be busy that day. With no shore visits to look forward to, there could be a number of people turning up at the surgery. She'd just decided to make an early start when there was a knock on her cabin door and she found Liam standing outside.

'I'm sorry to bother you so early in the day but we've got a bit of a problem, I'm afraid.'

'That sounds ominous,' she replied, summoning a smile.

Liam had been rather distant since they'd docked at Naples. She'd put it down to the fact that he was missing Julia because as far as she was aware the woman hadn't been in touch with him yet. However, the thought that his happiness was so bound up with someone else wasn't easy to accept.

'It is. We have six guests all complaining of sickness and diarrhoea, apparently. The captain has been on the phone to me and he's extremely concerned. The last thing he needs is an outbreak of food poisoning on board the ship.'

'I can imagine!' she exclaimed. 'It would cause chaos if a lot of passengers went down with it.'

'Exactly. Anyway, I'm on my way to see the passengers concerned now and I'd like you to come with me. The sooner we find out what's causing this, the faster we can take steps to deal with it. Gastroenteritis can run riot in this kind of environment.'

'I'm ready whenever you are. Just let me find my shoes... Where *did* I put them?' Sophie looked round the cabin, trying to remember where she'd last seen the white leather loafers that she wore with her uniform.

'Here they are.' Liam bent down and retrieved the missing footwear from the gap beneath the vanity unit. He offered them to her with a flourish. 'Cinderella *shall* go to the ball!'

Sophie laughed as she sat down on the stool to put them on. 'Some ball! You really know how to give a girl a good time, Liam Kennedy.'

'You help me sort out this problem and I'll treat you to the best night out you've ever had,' he promised, grinning at her.

'Hmm, don't think I won't hold you to that either,' she warned, before it struck her that the likelihood of them having a night out together was very slim. Once she left the ship, she doubted if she would ever see him again.

The thought was just too painful so Sophie quickly stood up and headed out of the door. 'Do you have their cabin numbers?' she said, hoping it would help if she focused on work.

Why was it so difficult to imagine never seeing Liam again when she'd got through the last two years without him? She'd thought her feelings for him had died a long time ago but if she felt nothing then why had she stood at the porthole last night, wishing they could try again?

'They're in adjoining staterooms on Pacific deck. Apparently, it's a group of friends who all got married around the same time and decided to celebrate their silver wedding anniversaries by coming on this cruise together.'

They reached the lift and he stopped to press the button. 'At least we won't have to go dashing from one end of the ship to the other.'

'Very handy, although I doubt they planned it that way for our convenience,' she pointed out, determined not to let him see there was anything wrong. She couldn't bear it if Liam guessed how mixed up she felt. He seemed to have his life sorted out and it wouldn't be fair to let him see how confused she was.

'I'm sure they didn't.' He laughed ruefully. 'A dose of gastroenteritis isn't the kind of anniversary present I'd look forward to after twenty-five years of marriage!'

Sophie didn't say anything. There was no point dwelling on the fact that at one time she'd been confident they would be celebrating an anniversary like that. When they had exchanged their marriage vows she'd meant them every bit as much as Liam had done. The thought was so poignant that her heart ached.

Mrs Davies looked worn out when she answered the door to them. Sophie had seen her about the ship on a number of occasions and it was difficult to equate the happy, smiling fifty-year-old with the wan-faced woman standing before them.

'I have never felt so ill in my entire life!' Monica Davies exclaimed, leading them into the spacious sitting room. 'I was sick so many times that I gave up counting in the end. And as for the rest... Well, the least said about *that*, the better.'

'It sounds as though you've had a nasty case of gastro-enteritis, Mrs Davies. I believe your husband has also been ill and your friends...' Liam glanced at the slip of paper he held '...Mr and Mrs Baxter and Mr and Mrs Shepherd?'

'That's right. But surely there've been other passengers complaining about feeling ill?' Monica said, frowning. 'It can't be just us six who've come down with this bug?'

'We've not had any more reports so far,' Liam explained gently. 'That's why I'm so keen to find out what has caused you and your friends to be ill.'

'What you really mean, Doctor, is that you want to stop folk finding out what's been going on. It wouldn't look good if word got out that the hygiene standards on board this ship aren't what they're supposed to be!'

Sophie swung round when Mr Davies suddenly appeared from the bedroom. He looked as worn out as his wife but it was obvious that he was also extremely angry. Her heart sank because the last thing they wanted was a confrontation when they needed to resolve this problem as fast as possible.

'It certainly wouldn't, Mr Davies. However, I'm less concerned about the reputation of the ship than I am about making sure you and your friends receive the very best possible care. That's the reason why I want to find out what has caused you all to be ill—so I can help you and prevent anyone else suffering the way you've done.'

Liam didn't raise his voice but he still managed to get his point across. Sophie saw Bill Davies's start of surprise. It was obvious the man hadn't expected that response from someone in authority yet it was typical of Liam. He'd always refused to play politics even when it might have furthered his career. He was too honest to compromise about the rights and wrongs of a situation for personal gain. It brought it home to her once again how wrong she'd been not to trust him.

'I'm sorry, Doctor. I was out of order, saying that.' Bill Davies sank down on the couch beside his wife and sighed. 'I'm just angry because this trip was meant to be such a special occasion and now it's completely ruined.'

'Nonsense!' Monica declared robustly. 'All right, so maybe last night was horrendous but look on the bright side, Bill. We'll be able to dine out on this tale for years to come!'

Everyone laughed. Bill put his arm around his wife and

hugged her. 'Now you can see why I love this woman so much, can't you? I wouldn't trade her for the world. People seem surprised when they learn that we've clocked up twenty-five years of marriage but it's quite simple, really. When you find the right woman, you should hang onto her, Dr Kennedy!'

'Sounds like good advice to me, Mr Davies.'

Sophie frowned when she heard the wistful note in Liam's voice. Maybe she was reading too much into it but it sounded almost as though he wished he'd held onto *her*.

Her head spun as she tried to make sense of it. Part of her was following the conversation as Liam explained to the Davieses that most cases of gastroenteritis were caused by bacteria contaminating the food and water supplies and that was why he needed to know everything they'd eaten and drunk in the past twenty-four hours. However, the rest of her mind was busily testing out the theory that Liam wanted her back in his life. Was it possible or was she simply attributing her own feelings to him?

Her breath caught because there was no way she could pretend any longer. She loved him *and* she wanted him back! It was as though a light had been switched on and she could see everything clearly for the first time in ages. She had never actually stopped loving him, just told herself she had because it had been easier than admitting how she really felt. But was it possible for dreams to come true a second time? Or was she simply setting herself up for more heartache?

'So you all ate breakfast in the dining-room then had coffee by the pool before you went ashore at Tunis? Did you have anything to eat with your coffee?'

Liam forced himself to concentrate as Monica explained that she and the two other women in their party had had Danish pastries but their husbands had drunk only coffee. He moved on to lunch—a packed lunch provided by the chef for all the passengers who were going on the trip to a local market—but it wasn't easy to keep his mind on the conversation. He wasn't sure what was wrong with Sophie but there was definitely something amiss because he could feel the vibes that were winging his way. He glanced at her and felt his heart bang against his ribs when he saw the expression on her face. She looked both shocked and elated, but why?

It was impossible to work out the answer when he needed to concentrate on what Mr and Mrs Davies were saying. However, he promised himself that he would find out what was going on the moment he had a chance. There was probably no basis for this feeling of excitement that was building inside him but there was no way he intended to ignore it.

'And you didn't eat anything while you were at the souk? You're quite sure?' he insisted. 'I know how tempting it is to try some of these local dishes but buying food from market stalls is one of the fastest ways to contract food poisoning. Food that has been left uncovered in the heat can harbour umpteen different bacteria.'

'No, nothing at all. Rose—that's Mrs Baxter—warned us not to eat anything. She lived abroad for a while so knows all about the dangers,' Monica explained. 'We just had a drink before the bus arrived to take us back to the harbour.'

'What did you have to drink?' Liam put in, immediately picking up on that point.

'Just bottled water, Dr Kennedy,' Bill assured him. 'We were all parched so we bought some mineral water off this young boy who was selling it near to where we'd arranged to be picked up.'

'And did you check the bottles to make sure the seals weren't broken?' he asked.

'Well, no. I never gave it a thought, did you, Monica?' Bill frowned when his wife shook her head. 'I can't see how there was anything wrong with the water, Dr Kennedy, if that's what you're suggesting. It was a well-known brand, one we buy from the supermarket at home, in fact.'

'It's possible the water in the bottles wasn't actually mineral water,' Liam explained gently, inwardly sighing because far too many tourists were caught out that way. 'The street vendors collect empty mineral-water bottles from rubbish bins and refill them with local tap water. It's fine if you're used to drinking it, but it's not nearly so good for delicate foreign constitutions.'

'I can't believe we fell for it!' Bill sounded mortified. 'It was my idea to buy the water off the boy, too, because I felt sorry for him.'

'We can't be sure it was the water,' Liam warned him, although he had a feeling it would turn out to be the culprit. 'We'll have to wait and see if anyone else has been affected by this bug first.'

'I doubt it. We were the first ones to get back to the meeting point because we'd seen all we wanted to by that point. The boy had gone by the time the others arrived,' Bill explained.

'Well, let's hope you're right. In the meantime, I'm afraid there's not much I can do other than to advise you both to drink plenty of fluids—water for the first twenty-four hours and maybe a little fruit juice after that. Also, you need to rest. You're bound to feel washed out but the sickness and diarrhoea will gradually subside.'

He smiled sympathetically when Monica groaned. 'I know it's not the best way to end your holiday but look on the bright side—it might have happened at the beginning of the trip! Anyway, either Sophie or I will pop in throughout the day to check that you're all right. Hopefully, you'll be feeling better by this time tomorrow but call me if you are at all concerned or if your symptoms get any worse.'

Liam made sure they had the phone number of the surgery then he and Sophie went to visit the two other couples. He explained his suspicions about the water, offered the same advice he'd given to the Davieses and assured them that he or Sophie would visit them during the day. It all took some time and he frowned as he checked his watch as they got back into the lift.

'It's too late for breakfast now. We'll need to open the surgery in half an hour's time. Why don't I pop to the LiteBite Café and fetch us back some coffee and doughnuts? I don't know about you but I'm starving.'

'That sounds like a good idea,' she agreed immediately.

The lift arrived at their deck and she went to get out, but Liam stopped her. He could feel his heart racing but he simply couldn't wait any longer to find out what was going on.

'And while we're eating maybe you can tell me what's on your mind, Sophie.'

'I don't know what you mean,' she denied at once, but he'd seen the betraying colour that had swept up her face.

'Don't you?' He looked her straight in the eye. 'Something happened while we were talking to the Davieses. I don't know what it was all about but I could sense there was something bothering you and I'd like to know what it is.'

He touched her lightly on the cheek, feeling his heart

fill with tenderness when he saw the shock in her eyes. In that second he knew he wouldn't rest until he found out the truth because if there was a chance that Sophie felt something for him then he had to make her tell him before it was too late.

She didn't say anything more as she hurriedly got out of the lift. Liam pressed the button then took a deep breath as the lift whisked him to Atlantic deck. He needed to compose himself so he could focus on whatever Sophie had to tell him, but it was hard to remain calm when the truth was clamouring to make itself heard.

He loved Sophie *and* he wanted her back!

There was no way he could pretend about his feelings any longer because he didn't have the time. She would be going out of his life for good in less than forty-eight hours' time if he didn't find a way to stop her. He only hoped and prayed she felt the same about him but he would have to wait and see. It was all down to her now, to how *she* felt about *him*.

Liam groaned because he had *never* planned on this happening. The only reason he'd wanted to see Sophie again had been so he could finalise his plans for the future. Now everything was up in the air. He had no idea what Sophie was going to tell him and even less idea how she would react if he told her he loved her. Every single aspect of his life seemed to be peppered with doubts...

Except one.

If he did get her back then he would never, *ever* make the mistake of letting her go again!

CHAPTER ELEVEN

SOPHIE paced the floor, wondering what she was going to tell Liam when he came back. He'd sounded so determined to find out what was bothering her and she had no idea what she was going to say...

She sighed because how could she tell him that she loved him when she had no idea of the repercussions it might cause? Maybe it *had* sounded as though he regretted their divorce but it would be foolish to read too much into it. He was planning to marry Julia and, so far as she was aware, nothing had changed.

'Coffee and doughnuts coming right up!'

Liam backed into the room, balancing two Styrofoam cups of coffee on top of a large box of doughnuts. Sophie hurriedly took the drinks from him and put them on the desk.

'Thanks.' He opened the box and offered it to her. 'I wasn't sure which were your favourites so I asked for a selection.'

'They look lovely. Thank you.' Sophie dipped into the box and took a chocolate frosted doughnut. She wasn't really hungry but at least it delayed her having to say anything. Should she tell Liam the truth or should she lie to him? Either option seemed fraught with problems.

'Try a different one if you don't fancy that one. There's plenty to choose from.'

She jumped when he spoke, only then realising that she'd been staring at the doughnut without making any attempt to eat it. 'No, this is fine. Really,' she said hurriedly.

She took a bite of the sweet confection but it was hard to swallow it when her throat seemed to have closed up with nerves. When Liam reached over and took the doughnut from her, she didn't protest. He dropped it into the waste bin then passed her a paper napkin.

'The trouble with doughnuts is that they make your hands really sticky, don't they?' he said conversationally. However, Sophie had seen the searching look he'd given her and her heart started to race. Any moment now Liam was going to ask her to explain what was worrying her and she still had no idea what she was going to tell him.

'Still, it's worth a bit of mess for the enjoyment you get out of them. That applies to a lot of things in life, doesn't it? You have to deal with the messy bits before you get to the good parts.'

His tone was so gentle that her eyes filled with tears. He was doing his best to reassure her and it made it all the more difficult to know what to do. He'd already admitted how guilty he felt about the way he'd handled things after Zoë had died so was she really prepared to take the risk of him sacrificing his own happiness for hers?

She knew him too well, knew how difficult he would find it to hurt her a second time. However, for a relationship to work, both people needed to be totally committed to each other. She couldn't bear to think that he might ask her to go back to him out of pity rather than love.

'That's very true,' she agreed, her heart aching because she really didn't have a choice. She had to convince Liam that she didn't need him and in that way set him free to get on with his life. It wouldn't be easy because he was already suspicious, but there might be a way—if she could pull it off.

'At least we've got all the messy bits in our lives sorted out at last. It should be all good from here on.'

'Sounds as though you've made some plans,' he observed, leaning against the desk while he sipped his coffee.

'I have. It was one of those light-bulb moments—d'you know what I mean? The answer to your problems comes to you in a blinding flash.' She laughed, hoping he couldn't tell that her heart was breaking. 'No wonder you thought I looked a bit strange while we were talking to the Davieses!'

'I see. You'd just had some kind of revelation, had you?'

He raised the cup to his lips and Sophie felt her insides twist when she saw that his hand was shaking. Was he nervous about what she was going to say, worried about the repercussions it might have? The thought gave her the strength to continue because she couldn't and *wouldn't* do anything to hurt him when she loved him so much.

'You could call it that, although it's something I've thought about quite a lot in the past. I've decided to retrain and go in for midwifery. I always fancied doing it but I kept putting it off for all sorts of reasons. Now seems like the perfect time to take the plunge.'

'I remember you mentioning that you were interested in becoming a midwife shortly before we found out you were expecting Zoë,' he said quietly.

'That's right,' she agreed, desperate to convince him that she was telling the truth. Maybe it wasn't such a bad idea after all. It made sense to have a complete break from the work she'd always done and what could be better than helping to bring new lives into the world? Her heart lifted just a little because it was a relief not to have to tell him a total lie.

'Once I realised I was pregnant then everything changed because it wasn't the right time to think about retraining. As for the past couple of years, well, it was simply easier to carry on doing a job I knew.'

'But now you've decided it's time you made a fresh start? Is that what you're saying, Sophie?'

'Yes, that's it exactly. Taking this job was the first step, of course, but even then I wasn't sure what I was going to do after my contract ended.' She shrugged. 'I know I claimed that I might go abroad to work but I'm not sure I would have actually done it if push came to shove. It would have been too tempting to go back to what I knew, but now everything has changed. And I have you to thank for that, Liam.'

'Me? How do you work that out?'

He put his cup on the desk and she felt her breath catch when she saw the bleakness in his eyes. Why did he look so *devastated*? she wondered sickly. Had he been hoping that she would tell him something other than the fact that she'd decided on a change of career?

Sophie's mind veered away from that tantalising thought because she couldn't allow herself to go down that route again. He loved Julia. He must do because he was going to marry her. Those were the facts and there was no basis whatsoever for thinking that he wanted *her* back.

'Because if you hadn't taken this job with the express intention of sorting out the mistakes we made two years ago, I might never have reached this point.' She summoned a smile but it was one of the hardest things she'd ever had to do, to smile when her heart was breaking.

'Thank you, Liam. I suppose the best way to describe

what you've done for me is to say that you've set me free.
I can put the past behind me at last and start living again!'

Liam wasn't sure how he managed to contain himself. He
wanted to rant and rail at fate for the cruel trick it had
played on him. *He'd* been the one who'd wanted to free
himself from the past! *He'd* been the one to take this job
so he could get on with his life! Now he had no idea what
the future held in store for him, apart from the fact that
Sophie wouldn't feature in it. The thought almost brought
him to his knees.

'Then all I can say is that I'm glad everything has
worked out so well for you.' He cleared his throat when
he heard the ache in his voice because the last thing he
wanted was to spoil things when she sounded so happy.
'At least something good has come out of all this and
that's the main thing.'

'It has and it's all thanks to you, Liam.'

She smiled at him, a brilliant, carefree smile that tore
holes in what little remained of his composure. There obviously wasn't a doubt in her mind about this decision
she'd made and it hurt unbearably to know that she could
cut him out of her life like this.

Liam's spirits were hovering somewhere around ground
level as he went into the consulting room. He sat down
at the desk, thinking about what had happened and what
it meant. Sophie had drawn that imaginary line under the
past that he'd once planned on doing and it was hard to
deal with the thought that their paths were unlikely to
cross again in the future. She would go her way and as
for him... Well, he had no idea what he was going to do.
The future suddenly loomed before him and there wasn't
a single thing he could find to look forward to.

*   *   *

It was a busy morning but Liam was glad because it meant he had less time to brood. He dealt with several cases of sunburn, a couple of muscle strains caused by too much sightseeing and then prescribed antihistamine cream for an elderly man who had a nasty insect bite on the back of his leg.

The whole area was very red and swollen so Liam advised him to bathe it in tepid water then apply the cream several times a day to counteract the irritation caused by the insect's saliva. After that there was a young woman who'd slipped getting out of the swimming pool and twisted her ankle. Her boyfriend brought her into the surgery and they were both dripping wet when they arrived.

He asked Sophie to fetch some towels while he took them into the consulting room. Fortunately, the ankle was sprained rather than broken so he explained that ice packs and paracetamol would help to alleviate the pain. Sophie applied a Tubigrip stocking for support and he advised the girl not to put any weight on the ankle for a couple of days, advice that was met by a marked lack of enthusiasm.

Liam sighed as Sophie saw the young couple out because he didn't hold too many hopes that the girl would follow his instructions. With the end of the cruise in sight, most people were eager to make the most of their final days on the ship. The best he could hope for was that she wouldn't make the injury any worse than it already was.

He left Sophie to deal with the paperwork while he went to check on the Davieses and their friends after surgery ended. Thankfully, all three couples reported an improvement in their condition, which was encouraging. There'd been no further reports of passengers being struck down so he phoned the captain and informed him that it

seemed unlikely the guests had contracted the bug on
board ship.

It was obviously a great relief to the captain because
he was fulsome in his thanks as he invited Liam to join
him in his cabin for drinks the following evening. He
included Sophie in the invitation and Liam promised to
pass on the message to her before he hung up.

He sighed as he sank back in the chair. Just two more
nights before Sophie left the ship. He only hoped he
would get through them without disgracing himself.

Sophie had decided to wear the grey chiffon dress again
on the Friday evening. Drinks with the captain would be
followed by a gala buffet dinner served on the promenade
deck. The passengers were due to leave the ship straight
after breakfast the following morning so it would be the
last big celebration for them.

Nobody had turned up for surgery that morning. The
ship had docked at Mahon and most passengers had decided to spend their last day ashore. She had filled in the
time as best she could but there'd been very little to do.
When Liam had suggested they should shut the surgery
early she had readily agreed.

She'd gone straight to her cabin and packed her suitcase
then spent the rest of the day there. It had seemed safer
to stay tucked away rather than run the risk of bumping
into Liam. Knowing how little time they had left together
was too difficult to deal with. She was terrified that she
would do something stupid, like blurting out that she
loved him, and it wouldn't be fair. She had to stick to her
decision to let Liam get on with his life, no matter how
painful it was going to be.

She paid one last visit to Monica and Bill Davies before
she got ready for dinner that night. Although they were

feeling a lot better that day, they certainly weren't well enough to join in the festivities. However, when she arrived at their suite, she discovered that Monica had organised her own party for her husband and their friends. Sophie couldn't help laughing when she saw the array of bottled waters and fruit juices Monica had ordered to celebrate the last night of their holiday. She ended up staying there far longer than she'd planned and consequently wasn't quite ready when Liam knocked on her door to escort her to the captain's cabin.

She quickly fastened the zipper on her dress and groaned when it jammed halfway up. No matter how hard she tried, she simply couldn't budge it. Holding the front of the dress against her, she went to the door.

'I'm almost ready,' she said, trying to control the surge her heart gave when she saw how handsome Liam looked. He was wearing a dinner jacket again that night and there was no doubt that the formal clothes suited him. It was an effort to keep the awareness out of her voice as she explained her predicament.

'The wretched zip has stuck and I can't seem to shift it. I don't want to make you late, so you go on ahead while I change into something else.'

'There's plenty of time yet. Let me see if I can sort it out.' He grinned as he flexed his fingers. 'I don't think a zip should present too many problems after some of the complicated surgery I've performed recently.'

'Don't count your chickens, hotshot!' she retorted.

'Oh, ye of little faith! When have I ever let you down?'

'Never,' she said huskily, because it was true. Liam had never let her down even though at one time she'd believed he had, and it was just so poignant to be reminded of that now.

'Then what are you waiting for? Turn round and let Dr Fixit solve the problem.'

Sophie did as she was told and turned so that her back was towards him. She bit her lip when she felt his knuckles brush her spine as he gently tugged at the zip. It was pure torture to feel him touching her like that and not be able to respond.

'It looks as though a thread has got caught between the teeth of the zip. Hold still while I see if I can snap it off,' he instructed.

Sophie flinched when she felt his breath suddenly cloud on the nape of her neck as he bent forwards. She could feel the warmth seeping into her body and shuddered convulsively. Her pulse began to beat in heavy, jerky thuds when she felt his hands suddenly grow still.

'Are you cold, Sophie?' His voice seemed to grate ever so slightly and she shivered again when she felt the vibrations from it running along her sensitised nerves.

'I…um…just a little.'

'That's strange because you don't feel cold.' He laid the back of his hand against her neck. 'In fact, I'd say you feel rather warm. I hope you aren't sickening for something.'

'I'm fine,' she assured him hastily, because the feel of his hand on her skin was making her body temperature rise even more. She hunted round for an explanation so that he wouldn't guess what was really going on. 'I've only just got out of the shower so I expect that's why I'm feeling a bit chilly. It's rather cool in here, isn't it?'

'I hadn't noticed but, then, I'm wearing a jacket. D'you want me to turn down the air-conditioning? Maybe that would help.'

'No, it's OK. I'll be fine.'

'Sure?'

He gave her a moment to reconsider then returned his attention to the zip. Sophie bit her lip when it struck her how close she'd come to giving herself away. What would Liam think if he realised the effect he had on her? she wondered sickly. Would he be shocked because it wasn't what he wanted?

Tears welled to her eyes because it was all such a mess. If only she'd realised how difficult he had found it to deal with his grief after Zoë had died, they might never have reached this point. They might still be together if she hadn't been such a fool. The thought seemed to pierce straight through the centre of her heart.

'I think I've got it... Yes!' He let out a cheer as he zipped up her dress.

Sophie hurriedly blinked away her tears before she turned. She had to deal with the situation as it stood and not keep torturing herself with 'what ifs'. She'd made a terrible mistake by not trusting him two years ago and now she had to live with the consequences. 'Thanks. I was dreading having to find something else to wear. My clothes are all packed and I expect they're creased to rags by now.'

'It would have been a real shame if you'd had to change. That dress really suits you, Sophie. You look lovely tonight.'

'Why, thank you kindly, sir!' She dropped him a mocking curtsey then quickly picked up her bag because there was no way she could keep up the pretence. In a few hours' time she and Liam would part for good and the thought was almost too much to bear. She just had to hold onto the thought that she was doing the right thing because now he would be free to find the happiness he deserved.

Her heart was heavy as they made their way to the

captain's quarters because it wasn't easy to accept that Liam would spend his life with another woman. A steward met them at the door and offered them drinks. Sophie took a glass of white wine off the tray then made her way into the drawing room. The captain was waiting to receive them so she and Liam stopped to speak to him. He thanked them both for their help during the recent crisis then asked her why she was leaving the ship.

She made some excuse but it was a relief when more guests arrived and they could make their escape. She glanced at Liam as they crossed the room and frowned when she saw the grim expression on his face. It was obvious there was something bothering him, but before she could ask him what was wrong, Mike Soames called him over.

Sophie left the two men talking and carried on. Several people spoke to her and she did her best to respond but her heart really wasn't in it. She couldn't stop thinking about how little time she had left with Liam. It had been bad enough when they'd first split up but the thought of them parting now was so much worse. Now there was no anger to buoy her up, just a deep sense of loss gnawing away inside her. It was a relief when Yuri suddenly appeared at her side and provided a distraction.

'I am so disappointed, Sophie! Why didn't you tell me that you were leaving tomorrow? I have only just heard the news and I am desolate because I thought we were friends.'

'Of course we're friends,' she said quickly. She felt quite guilty about the oversight, although it was understandable when she'd had so much on her mind of late. 'And I'm sorry I didn't tell you but it wasn't intentional, you understand. I just never seemed to find the right moment.'

'Ah, I see. You were worried in case I was upset?'

Yuri lifted her hand to his lips and tenderly kissed it. Sophie inwardly sighed because he'd completely misunderstood. However, it seemed easier to let it pass so she didn't bother correcting him.

'Of course I'm upset, Sophie. I'd hoped that you and I would have the chance to get to know one another better, but these things happen.' He treated her to an intimate little smile. 'And we still have tonight to enjoy each other's company, don't we? That is some small consolation.'

'I…um…yes,' Sophie murmured, her heart sinking because the last thing she needed was to have to spend the night fending off his advances.

She quickly withdrew her hand as a couple of guests came over to speak to him, wondering how she could tactfully explain that she wasn't interested in him. She didn't want to be rude but neither did she want to encourage him when there was no point.

She glanced around the room, seeking inspiration, and felt her heart leap when she discovered that Liam was watching them. Just for a second their eyes held before he turned to reply to something Mike had said, but it was long enough to make every pulse in her body suddenly pound.

Sophie's head reeled as the blood rushed through her veins. She honestly thought she was going to faint and knew that she had to leave before she made a fool of herself. Yuri was still talking and he didn't notice her slipping away. She quickly left the captain's cabin and went out onto the deck, hoping that some fresh air would help. The staff had finished laying out the buffet and there were a few early diners already lining up to be served. When a waiter offered to find her a seat, she shook her head and carried on until she reached a secluded spot near the stern.

She leant against the rail and made herself take several deep breaths until the giddiness began to recede, but even then it was still impossible to make sense of what had happened. How could she explain why Liam should have been jealous when he'd seen Yuri paying her attention? He had Julia in his life now so why should he care what *she* did?

Unless he still felt something for her, of course.

Her heart began to pound as she stared at the vastness of the sea. Was it possible that Liam still loved her?

Liam wasn't sure how he managed to restrain himself. Watching that damned fellow making eyes at Sophie was almost more than he could bear! He wanted to go straight over there and order him to keep his hands off her, only he didn't have the right to interfere.

Pain ripped through him and he realised that he had to get away before he made a spectacle of himself. He made some excuse to Mike then left. The ship was gearing up for the night's festivities and suddenly the thought of being surrounded by people all intent on having fun was more than he could bear. Maybe it *was* part of his job to entertain the guests but to hell with duty for once. He needed some time on his own to come to terms with the fact that Sophie would never again be his!

His heart felt like lead as he made his way along the promenade deck. He bypassed the buffet, shaking his head when a waiter asked him if he was dining that night. He didn't want food—he wanted Sophie! He wanted to feel her in his arms, taste her mouth under his, breathe in her scent and savour her sweetness so he could feel whole again.

For the past two years he'd been existing rather than living, going through the motions because that was what had been expected of him. People didn't give up because they'd lost the one person who meant anything to them. They kept on breathing and eating, working and sleeping—getting through each day the best way they could.

He'd tried to tell himself that he'd got his life back on track when he'd met Julia but he'd been fooling himself. Julia hadn't been able to give him back all that he'd lost or put some purpose back into each and every day. Now the thought of having to carry on like that for however many years was unbearable, but he didn't have a choice. Sophie didn't want him, didn't need him, didn't love him. Period!

Liam had reached the stern and he ground to a halt when he suddenly spotted Sophie leaning against the rail. She looked so troubled and unhappy that he was immediately stricken with guilt. She'd obviously noticed the way he'd been glaring at Yuri and he cursed himself for not keeping a tighter rein on his feelings because it wasn't fair to upset her like this. She deserved to find happiness again, to find someone to love her and whom she could love in return. So maybe he didn't believe that damned purser was the right man for her but it wasn't up to him to make that kind of a decision. If Sophie was attracted to the fellow then he had no right to put *any* obstacles in her way!

'Looks like we've both had the same idea.' He summoned a smile when she swung round, feeling pain lance his heart when he saw her swiftly avert her eyes again. It hurt to know that she didn't welcome his company but he had to hold onto the thought that it was Sophie's happiness that mattered and nothing else.

'Did you fancy a bit of peace and quiet, too?' he continued, struggling to keep the ache out of his voice as he went over to join her.

'Something like that,' she agreed, still without looking at him.

Liam sighed because he knew he owed her an apology for the way he had behaved. 'Look, Sophie, I'm sorry about what happened earlier.' He shrugged when she looked sharply at him. 'I was totally out of order.'

'I don't know what you mean—' she began, but he didn't let her finish.

'Of course you do!' He grimaced when she jumped but it wasn't easy to contain his emotions. He was about to push the woman he loved into another man's arms and *nobody* could claim that it was an easy thing to do!

'Sorry again. I didn't mean to snap but it isn't easy for me to admit that I was jealous when I saw the way Yuri was making a play for you. However, we both know that it's got nothing to do with me what you do.'

'In that case, why should you be jealous?'

Liam frowned when he heard the terse note in her voice all of a sudden. He had the funniest feeling that his answer was really important to her, although for the life of him he couldn't work out what she wanted him to say...

Unless she wanted to be absolutely sure that he no longer felt anything for her?

His heart sank like a stone because it just seemed to fit so perfectly that he knew it must be true. Sophie had always been far too kind to hurt anyone. If she believed that he still harboured some feelings for her then she would avoid spending any more time with Yuri that night. He had to admit that the idea held a definite appeal, but would it be *fair* to ruin her evening because he couldn't handle the thought of her with another man?

'Habit, I guess.' He shrugged, praying that she couldn't

tell how awful he felt. He needed to convince her that he didn't care and it wasn't easy when it felt as though his heart was being passed through the meat grinder. 'I suppose I'm still programmed to feel a bit uptight whenever I see you with someone else.'

'I don't see why.' She stood up straighter and stared at him. 'We're divorced, Liam. You no longer need to feel responsible for me, if that's what you're saying.'

'I know that.' He shrugged when he saw the scepticism on her face. She obviously didn't believe him and he searched for something else that might convince her. Maybe a snippet of the truth would add weight to his story? It was worth a try.

'All right, then, I'll admit that I'm not convinced Yuri is the right guy for you, but I suppose that's for you to decide, Sophie, isn't it?'

'Yes, it is. How kind of you to acknowledge that fact, Liam.'

She sounded angry and he looked at her in dismay. 'I'm sorry. I didn't mean to upset you…'

'You didn't! Now, if you'll excuse me, it's time I got back.' She treated him to a grim little smile that could have stopped traffic. 'Yuri will be wondering where I've got to and I don't want to keep him waiting.'

'Of course not.'

Liam quickly stepped aside to let her pass. He had a horrible feeling that he hadn't handled things very well, although he wasn't sure what else he could have done. His mouth thinned when he saw Yuri hurry forward as soon as she appeared and place a proprietorial arm around her waist as he led her to a table. It looked as though Sophie's night was going to plan so there was no point in him hanging around.

He left the promenade deck and went back inside, using

the rear staircase so he could avoid the crowds of passengers who were arriving for the buffet. He would have an early night, he decided as he made his way to his cabin, catch up on some of the sleep he'd missed recently. Maybe he *should* be making an effort to entertain the guests but he definitely didn't want Sophie to think he was trying to cramp her style!

He cursed softly as he let himself into his cabin and stripped off his jacket. Tossing it over the chair, he lay down on his bunk. He could hear the strains of music coming from outside as the orchestra tuned up. Dinner was to be followed by dancing and he could imagine the fun everyone would have, dancing the night away under the stars. Sophie would definitely enjoy it because she loved dancing and tonight she would have such a willing partner…

Liam groaned because the thought of her in another man's arms was more than he could stand yet what could he do about it? He could hardly go back and tell her that he loved her when she'd made it clear it was the last thing she wanted to hear! He had to accept what was happening and not do anything to spoil the night for her. After all, there was just this one night to get through before she left the ship. Surely he could manage not to make a fool of himself for a few more hours?

CHAPTER TWELVE

'ARE you sure you won't change your mind, Sophie, and join me for a nightcap? It seems a shame to bring the evening to an end. I have a bottle of brandy in my cabin that I've been saving for a special occasion such as this.'

'It's very kind of you, Yuri, but it's late and I still have a lot to do.'

Sophie quickly pushed back her chair and stood up. The dancing had ended some time ago and most of the passengers were now making their way back to their cabins. She hadn't intended to stay so late but each time she'd tried to leave, Yuri had stopped her. Now, however, it was time she brought the evening to an end, even though it might not be the ending Yuri had in mind for it!

'My flight leaves at ten in the morning and I still have some packing to do,' she explained, glossing over the fact that she only needed to pop her toiletries into her case. 'I'll have to miss out on the nightcap, I'm afraid.'

'Sure?' He sighed soulfully when she nodded. 'In that case, I shall have to bow to the inevitable. However, there is one last thing before you go.'

He drew her into his arms and kissed her. Sophie didn't resist purely and simply because it didn't seem worth causing a scene. A wave of sadness washed over her when she felt his lips urging hers to respond. There was no doubt that Yuri was a skilful lover but he wasn't Liam and his kiss would never have the power to stir her.

He obviously sensed her lack of response because he abruptly released her. Sophie sighed when he bade her a

chilly goodnight. She hadn't meant to offend him but neither could she pretend. The truth was that she wasn't interested in any man except Liam.

Pain ripped through her and she pressed a hand to her
mouth to stifle a sudden sob. All evening long she had
tried to blot out the memory of that conversation they'd
had, but it had been impossible to forget it. If she'd
needed proof that Liam didn't feel anything for her then
she had it in spades. He didn't love her—he couldn't do
when he'd virtually *driven* her into another man's arms.

All of a sudden Sophie knew there was no way that she
dared go back to her cabin at the present moment and run
the risk of bumping into him. She had no idea where Liam
had gone after she'd left him, but there were still a lot of
people about. The thought of having to explain why she
was upset was more than she could bear. Did she really
want to take the chance of blurting out that she loved him
when it was something he wouldn't want to hear?

She quickly made her way up the steps to the sun terrace. There was nobody else there so she sat down on one
of the chairs beside the swimming pool. It was dark on
the deck with only the glow from the pool lights to dispel
the gloom, but it suited her mood. She didn't want bright
lights and laughter—she wanted time to compose herself.

Kicking off her shoes, she settled down in the chair.
She could hear the crew talking on the deck below as they
cleared away the buffet tables and the laughter of a few
boisterous revellers returning to their cabins but after a
while the noise stopped and peace settled over the ship.

She yawned widely as the events of the past few days
suddenly caught up with her, all the emotional turmoil
and heartache she'd been through. There was little chance
of her running into Liam if she went back to her cabin

now but she was just too comfortable to get up. Her eye-lids started to droop and a few seconds later she drifted off to sleep.

Liam couldn't sleep. He lay on his bunk, watching the minutes ticking away. Midnight came and went and there was still no sign of Sophie returning to her cabin. Where was she? The dancing had ended some time ago and he couldn't understand what was keeping her...

Unless she'd decided to spend the night with Yuri, of course.

He shot to his feet, unable to lie there while images of Sophie in another man's bed danced inside his head. It was one thing to tell himself that he wanted her to be happy and another thing entirely to face what it actually meant. He loved her! He needed her! And, by hell, he was going to tell her that before it was too late!

He left his cabin and strode along the passageway. He had no idea where the purser's cabin was situated, but the crew's quarters were two decks below so he would go down there and just knock on every door until he found the right one. Of course, Sophie might not be exactly thrilled about him turning up, but once he'd explained why he was there, she would understand...

Wouldn't she?

Doubt reared its ugly head but Liam ruthlessly stamped it down. He wasn't going to let anything come between him and Sophie ever again! He'd made that mistake once before and he wasn't going to let it happen a second time. He would find her, tell her that he loved her and some-how, some *way* make her see that they belonged together.

'If you're looking for Miss Patterson, Doc, she's on the sun terrace.'

Liam spun round when he heard Charlie's voice. 'The sun terrace?' he repeated uncertainly. 'Are you sure?'

'Yep. I spotted her just now when I was taking one of the guests some cocoa, and wondered what she was doing there on her own.'

Charlie grimaced as he tucked the silver salver under his arm. 'Let's hope it's the last order of the day, too, because I could do with some shut-eye.'

'I'm sure you could,' Liam replied distractedly, his mind racing. What was Sophie doing on the sun terrace at this time of the night? Why had she gone up there instead of going back to her cabin? It didn't make sense...unless something had happened.

His mouth settled into a grim line as he bade Charlie a hasty goodnight and ran towards the stairs. If Yuri had done anything to upset her, he wouldn't be responsible for his actions!

He took the stairs, two at a time, so that he was out of breath when he reached the sun terrace. He ignored the painful ache in his lungs, however, as he raced across the deck because he had more important things to worry about. He would never forgive himself for letting Sophie go off with that Yuri fellow if she'd been harmed in any way. He wanted to protect and cherish her, not put her at risk!

Liam ground to a halt when he suddenly saw her curled up on a deck chair beside the pool. She looked so small and defenceless that his heart began to beat in short, jerky bursts. He ran across the deck and knelt beside her, hearing the thunder of his own heartbeat drumming in his ears when she didn't acknowledge him in any way.

Why didn't she say something? he wondered frantically. Anything would do even if she only told him to go away. He just needed to be sure that she was all right...

A snore suddenly issued from her lips and Liam's head bowed in relief when he realised that she was fast asleep. Quite frankly, he didn't know whether to laugh or cry so ended up doing both because he'd been so afraid that something awful might have happened to her. The thought of Sophie coming to any harm made his legs go weak and his insides turn to mush and yet he knew that he would fight dragons if that was what it took to protect her! If he had to give up his life to keep her safe then he would do so without a second thought.

'Liam? What's wrong? What are you doing here? Are you ill or something?'

The bewilderment in her voice brought his head up and he looked at her with his heart in his eyes. Maybe he should have tried to hide his feelings for the moment but he just didn't have the strength. 'No, I'm not ill, sweetheart. I'm just so relieved that you're all right.'

'What do you mean? Of course I'm all right. Why shouldn't I be?' She pushed herself up in the chair and stared at him, her blue eyes filled with confusion and something else, something that made his heart start to race all over again. Liam took a deep breath to steady himself. Maybe he was looking for something that didn't really exist because he was so desperate, but he was past worrying about the rights and wrongs and all the nuances in between. He loved her! And he wanted her to know that before it was too late.

'I was worried when you didn't come back to your cabin. I was afraid that something might have happened to you.' He took her hand and pressed his lips to the centre of her palm as he looked into her eyes. 'I don't think I could carry on if anything happened to you, Sophie. I wouldn't have the strength. I love you too much, you see, and anything that hurts you hurts me more.'

'You love me…' she said, the colour ebbing from her face so fast that Liam thought she was going to faint and grabbed hold of her arms.

She swatted his hands away and he recoiled in shock when he saw the white-hot fury on her face. 'How dare you tell me that, Liam Kennedy? How dare you? You…you push me into another man's arms, tell me that you don't care a jot about me and then have the nerve to come out with a statement like that!'

Liam was dumbfounded because he'd simply never envisaged her reacting like this. He hunted round for something to say—a few soothing words which would calm her down—but it was impossible to dredge up anything appropriate so he gave up. Sometimes it was much, much easier to fall back on actions rather than find the right words.

He pulled her into his arms so fast that she gasped. He wouldn't normally have employed such caveman tactics but he was too desperate to worry about his lack of finesse. He had to convince Sophie that he'd meant what he'd said, prove to her that he loved her, and he couldn't think of a better way.

His mouth found hers with an instinct born out of need and he groaned as he was immediately enveloped by an overpowering sense of relief. This was what he'd been born to do, he realised, what his soul had been crying out for throughout the past two years. His whole world could end at this very moment and he wouldn't care. Nothing mattered so long as he had Sophie in his arms, her mouth under his, her heart beating as fast and as furiously as his…

And it *was* beating furiously. Definitely faster than might have been expected if she was merely angry with him.

Liam raised his head and felt his heart fill with joy

when he saw the expression in her eyes, all the love he'd
yearned to see. He bent and rubbed his lips against hers,
willing her to say the words he longed to hear.

'Is there something you want to tell me, sweetheart?'
he prompted, letting his mouth touch hers again so that
she could not only hear the words but feel them as well.
He smiled when he felt the tiny, betraying shiver that
raced through her. Whoever had said that all was fair in
love had been right because he would employ any tactics
if it meant he could get her back!

'There is absolutely nothing I want to say to you, Liam
Kennedy! Not one single word. You don't deserve to hear
it after what you've done,' she retorted, although he was
very much aware that she hadn't made any attempt to free
herself from his arms.

'I know that, sweetheart,' he said placatingly, brushing
her mouth with another achingly soft kiss. 'I was completely in the wrong and I promise on my honour that I
shall apologise later for all my misdemeanours, but can't
you find it in your heart to be kind to me now?'

'Why should I be kind after you told me that you didn't
love me?' she shot back, turning her face to the side so
that he couldn't reach her mouth.

'Because I thought I was doing the right thing. That's
the truth. Cross my heart and hope to die.' He made a
cross on her left breast, right above her heart, and smiled
when he felt her nipple tauten and push against his palm.
He didn't want to get overly confident at this stage but
he sensed she wasn't *quite* as offended as she'd claimed.

'That is my heart you're crossing, not yours!'

'I know.' His lips searched for hers again then settled
on the tiny mole at the corner of her mouth when they
failed to make satisfactory contact. He kissed it gently

then kissed it a second time because it was such fun to feel her trembling like that.

A feeling of complete and utter amazement suddenly swept over him because he had never imagined he'd use the word 'fun' again to describe his relationship with Sophie. It just seemed to prove how far they had come in the past two weeks and the thought spurred him on.

'I know I was wrong, Sophie, but my intentions were good. I didn't want to get in your way if you were attracted to Yuri.'

'Who says I'm not attracted to him?' she shot back, then trembled when he drew a lazy pattern around her eager nipple with the very tips of his fingers.

'Me. I do. You wouldn't be lying here like this if you felt anything for him,' he stated firmly. Maybe he should be taking things a step at a time, but he couldn't help feeling impatient to get the preliminaries out of the way so they could get down to what really mattered—putting their lives back together.

'So now you're an expert on relationships, are you? My, my, Liam, what a marvel you are. Not only a hot-shot surgeon but an agony uncle to boot!'

'No, I'm not an expert. If I had been then the past couple of years wouldn't have been so horrendous for both of us.'

He kissed her tenderly then drew back and looked at her because he needed her to understand that he was being absolutely serious now. Fun and laughter were all part of the joy of being in love but sometimes one had to state the facts so there could be no mistake about what was meant. He didn't want there to be any mistake about what he was saying now.

'I can't ever give you back the two years we've lost but I can spend the next fifty-odd trying to make up for them if you'll let me. Will you? Do you think that you could ever find it in your heart to love me again just a little bit?'

Sophie bit her lip when she heard the pleading note in Liam's voice. She was so overwhelmed by joy that she couldn't speak. It felt as though all her birthdays and Christmases had come at once, as though every wish she'd ever had was about to be granted...

She jumped when Liam suddenly stood up, feeling the cold finger of fear sliding down her spine when she saw the set expression on his face. 'What's wrong?' she demanded, but he shook his head.

'Nothing's wrong. Please, don't feel bad, Sophie. I should never have asked you that. I shouldn't have tried to make you say something you don't—'

'For heaven's sake, Liam, shut up!'

She scrambled to her feet, ignoring his gasp at the way she'd spoken to him. She had no idea where her shoes had gone, which was a shame because she could have done with them when he was towering over her like the Grim Reaper. She quickly climbed onto the chair, sighing as she wondered how two supposedly intelligent human beings could make such a mess of things.

'Let's get this straight, Liam. Nobody can make me say something I don't mean, not even you.'

'I wasn't implying—' he began stiffly, but she put her fingers against his lips.

'Shh. Let me finish, darling. I promise you can talk all you like after I've had my say.' She smiled into his startled grey eyes. 'If you will really want to waste time talking, of course.'

She heard the click his throat made as he swallowed but he didn't utter a word, obviously deciding that it would be wiser to follow her instructions to the letter.

Sophie hid her smile because it wasn't like Liam to be so passive. She may as well make the most of it while it lasted.

'I love you, Liam. I always have loved you and I always shall love you. I made a terrible mistake by not trusting you two years ago but I hope and pray that we have sorted it all out now.'

She took her hand away from his mouth, tipping her head to the side as she looked at him enquiringly. 'That's all I wanted to say so the rest is up to you. I'm all ears.'

'I... You... We... Come here!'

He swept her into his arms, lifting her bodily off the chair and swinging her round until she was dizzy and clinging to him. Sophie laughed with sheer delight at his exuberance then sighed when he suddenly bent and kissed her, a kiss of such tenderness that her heart overflowed with happiness.

He gently set her back on her feet and looked into her eyes. 'I love you, Sophie Patterson. You are everything I have ever wanted. Maybe you should have trusted me but I should have tried harder to explain what had happened that night I stayed at Amanda's flat.'

'We were both too upset about Zoë to think clearly at the time,' she said softly, her eyes filling with tears at the memory of their precious child.

'We were,' he said with a catch in his voice. 'It was such an awful thing to happen, sweetheart, but we can try again if it's what you want.'

'You mean we can have another baby?' she said slowly, testing out the idea because she had never even considered it before.

'Yes, but only if it's what you want.' He framed her face between his hands and looked at her with his heart in his eyes. 'I just want you to be happy, Sophie. That's all.'

'I never thought I could feel this happy again,' she admitted. 'I thought I'd lost any chance of finding happiness when I lost you.'

She reached up and kissed him on the mouth. 'I love you, Liam, and maybe one day we can think about having another child, not to replace Zoë because it isn't possible to replace her. But it would be wonderful to have someone else who could share our love, wouldn't it?'

'Then that's what we'll do when the time feels right.' He kissed her back, letting the kiss set the seal on their promise.

Sophie shuddered as passion rose swiftly inside her when she felt his tongue teasing her lips to part for him. She moaned softly as she opened her mouth and felt his tongue dart inside. It was unbearably moving to have him kiss her like this after the long abstinence they'd endured, and she clung to him when he tried to draw back.

Liam obviously understood her frustration because he rained a shower of kisses over her face and neck. 'I desperately want to make love to you, Sophie, but I can't.'

'What do you mean, "can't"?' she said uncertainly, staring at him in surprise.

'That there's Julia to consider.' He rested his forehead against hers and she felt the tremor that ran through him. It was some small consolation because the mention of the other woman's name had filled her with dread but Liam swiftly allayed her fears.

'I can't make love to you until I've told Julia that I can't marry her. I expect it sounds ridiculously old-fashioned, but it just wouldn't feel right. You do understand, don't you, darling?'

'Of course I understand!' She smiled radiantly at him,

loving him even more for sticking to his principles. 'And I don't think it's ridiculous at all but just typical of the person you are, Liam.' She sighed sadly. 'I only hope Julia won't be too upset when you break the news to her.'

'I don't think it will come as too big a shock to her.' He grimaced when Sophie looked at him in surprise. 'I think Julia sensed that I had doubts, which was why she didn't object when I told her that I intended to see you again. I just wish I'd been able to reach her earlier then I could have got everything sorted out by now.'

'So you've known for some time that you loved me?' she asked softly.

'Yes. That's why I tried to phone Julia when we anchored at Naples.'

'But that was ages ago!' she exclaimed in surprise. 'Why didn't you say something sooner?'

'Why didn't you?' he countered, grinning as he dropped a kiss on her nose.

'Because I thought you didn't love me and I didn't want to ruin all your future plans.'

'Ditto!' He put his arms around her waist and pulled her to him, letting her feel his need for her in every tense muscle of his body. 'We're a fine pair of idiots, aren't we? We should have been brave enough to admit how we felt and saved ourselves a great deal of heartache!'

'Mmm, it's easy to be wise *after* the event.' She looped her arms around his neck and leant against him, smiling when she heard him groan. 'Now, now, Dr Kennedy. Remember all those high-minded principles of yours...'

She didn't get a chance to finish as his mouth swooped down and claimed hers. The kiss lasted quite some time so that she'd forgotten what she'd been saying when Liam raised his head, a fact he wasn't slow to remark on.

'What were you saying, Miss Patterson?' he teased, a wicked gleam in his eyes.

'I've no idea,' she admitted. 'I tend to get sidetracked when I'm kissed like that.'

'Really? I must make a note of that for future reference.' He dropped another deliciously sexy kiss on her mouth then reluctantly let her go. 'Anyhow, bearing in mind all those principles of mine, I suppose I shall have to behave with a bit more propriety from now on. That means we can rule out spending the night in your cabin or mine, so how about we spend it here instead?'

He swept a hand around the moonlit deck. 'How do you fancy spending the first night of the rest of our lives under the stars?'

'I can't think of anything I'd like more,' she said softly with a lump in her throat. When he opened his arms, she stepped into them and looked up at him with all the love she felt clear to see on her face.

'I love you so much, Liam. I know I've told you that already but I want to tell you again and again so you don't have any doubts that I mean it.'

'And I love you, too, Sophie.' He tilted her face up to his and tears filled her eyes when she saw that he was also crying. 'I promise that I won't let a day pass when I don't tell you that. I just feel so lucky to have got you back. There's just one thing that will make me even happier, if you'll agree to it.'

'Anything!' she declared recklessly.

'Promise that you will marry me just as soon as we can make the arrangements.' He sank down onto the chair and drew her down beside him. 'I don't want to waste any more time before I make you mine again!'

Sophie laughed as she dashed away her tears. 'I'll marry you tomorrow if you can sort it all out, Liam.'

'I'll keep you to that,' he growled, and kissed her.

'With the power vested in me I now pronounce you man and wife. You may kiss the bride!'

Sophie laughed as a great cheer erupted when Liam swept her into his arms. She kissed him back, wondering if she would wake up soon and find that she'd been dreaming because it was difficult to believe what had happened in the past few hours.

She and Liam had spent the night on the deck, talking a little, kissing a lot. Then, as soon as the sun had come up, Liam had insisted that she should go to her cabin and try to get some sleep. She hadn't thought she would be able to sleep after everything that had happened but she'd dropped off as soon as her head had touched the pillow.

She had been woken several hours later when Charlie had knocked on her door with a tray bearing a glass of champagne and a single, red rose. That had been just the first of a series of wonderful surprises, she had discovered, when Liam had arrived a few minutes later and calmly informed her that they would be married that very morning on the ship. The captain had agreed to preside over the ceremony, although there would also be an official from Palma present to make sure the ceremony was legal.

Sophie hadn't known what to say because she'd been so stunned by the speed of events. But when Liam had sat down on the bed and quietly explained that he had spoken to Julia and that she had given them her blessing, it had removed the final obstacle. Her heart had started racing when she'd realised that in less than an hour's time she would be Mrs Liam Kennedy again. The only problem had been what to wear but Liam had solved that by asking her to wear the grey dress that she'd worn the night before. She'd understood perfectly when he'd explained that he couldn't think of anything better for her to wear than the dress she'd had on when they had finally declared their love for each other...

'Happy?' Liam drew back and looked at her and she laughed when she saw the love in his eyes.

'Very happy.'

She stood on tiptoe and kissed him then grinned when another cheer rang around the deck. The passengers had soon got wind of what was happening and had thrown themselves into the proceedings with great enthusiasm. Gloria and Randolph Walters had even cancelled their flight so they could be at the wedding. Sophie smiled when she looked round and saw Gloria waving to her. She waved back then slid her arm through Liam's as the captain offered his congratulations.

Everyone started to disperse soon after that. The guests had to hurry to their cabins to finish packing and the crew had to prepare for the new intake of guests who would arrive that afternoon. Sophie sighed as they made their way below because she would have to leave the ship very shortly. She hated the thought of leaving Liam but there was nothing she could do about it. Her replacement would be on her way and her cabin would be needed for the newcomer.

'Not having regrets about marrying me already, I hope?' Liam demanded, pulling her into his arms as soon as they were safely inside his cabin. He kissed her long and lingeringly then grinned at her. 'I might be able to find a way to convince you that you've done the right thing if I really put my mind to it.'

'Sounds tempting,' she murmured, reaching up to nibble the edge of his jaw. 'The problem is that I don't have any doubts at all. Sorry!'

'Don't be sorry. It was a good answer and you deserve

a reward for it.' He kissed her again, even more thoroughly, and groaned. 'What you do to my libido, Mrs Kennedy, is simply amazing!'

'I'm pleased to be of service,' she replied pertly, then gasped when he swept her up in his arms and deposited her on the narrow bunk bed.

'What are you doing?' she demanded, laughing up at him. 'There isn't time for that now. I'm supposed to be leaving the ship!'

'You really think I'm going to let you leave when we've just got married?' Liam shook his head as he went to the door and turned the key. 'No way! I am not letting you out of my sight.'

'Well, obviously, I don't *want* to leave but how on earth can I stay when the agency is sending out a replacement for me?' she protested, her stomach churning with excitement when he came back and sat on the edge of the bed. It was an effort to carry on when she saw the way he was looking at her. 'The new nurse will need my cabin, Liam, and I know for a fact that the ship is fully booked because Charlie told me—'

'Has anyone ever told you that you talk too much, Sophie Kennedy?' He dropped a kiss on her mouth then smiled at her in such a way that she couldn't possibly have objected to the accusation. 'Everything is sorted out, sweetheart. I had a word with the captain and he has very kindly agreed to let us share this cabin.'

'Really?'

'Really.' He laughed when she gasped. 'I don't expect you ever imagined you'd be spending your honeymoon night squeezed into a single bunk bed, but do you think you could put up with it for my sake? I don't fancy being clapped in irons for jumping ship, but as there is no way that I intend to sail off into the sunset tonight without you, I'm prepared to take that risk.'

'Don't you dare! I don't care how cramped it is just so long as we can be together.' She wrapped her arms around his neck and pulled him down beside her. 'So now all that is sorted out, and you aren't going to be spending time in the brig, what happens next? Do you have any more plans?'

'Oh, yes. Loads of them. I'm planning on finding us that cottage in the country you always dreamed of, although I'll need to find a job first to pay for it…'

'It all sounds wonderful, darling, but what I *really* meant was do you have any plans for the rest of the day?'

'I was just coming to that. And, yes, I do have plans for today. In fact, they all centre on just one subject—you!'

Liam's mouth was urgent when it closed over hers but hers was just as hungry. They kissed for a long time until kissing wasn't enough. Sophie felt desire flow through her when Liam quickly stripped off his clothes then knelt beside the bunk and tenderly undressed her. With every touch of his hands he was telling her that he loved her, with each caress he was promising that he would always love her.

She knew how much this meant to him because it meant as much to her. At one time she had believed it would never happen yet when he held her against his heart as their bodies joined, she suddenly knew that their coming together again had been pre-ordained. She and Liam had been meant to be together for all eternity.

'I love you, Sophie,' he whispered just a moment before the world exploded in a shower of stars.

'And I love you, too,' she whispered. 'So much…'

EPILOGUE

Two years later…

'STOP him, Liam! Don't let him get out into the garden or he'll be covered in mud again!'

'Oh, no, you don't, young man!' Liam laughed when his small son gurgled with delight as he swept him up into the air. He carried the child back inside the house, pausing to drop a kiss on Sophie's lips and another on the blonde curls of the baby girl clinging to her legs.

The twins had become a real handful since they had started walking and he didn't know how Sophie coped with them while he was at work. He had to admit that they wore him out but he wouldn't have swapped them for the world.

Jack and Martha were living, breathing proof of the love he and Sophie felt for one another, and he'd been ecstatic when they'd found out she'd been expecting twins. They had found the cottage they had always dreamed about and had settled in Dalverston after he'd been offered a job at the hospital there. Sophie had finished her midwife's training and now worked two days a week in the antenatal unit. There was a crèche at the hospital for the twins so everything had worked out really well. Not for the first time, Liam thought how lucky he was. Few people got a second chance at happiness and he didn't know why he'd been so blessed.

He put Jack down and took Sophie in his arms as the twins toddled off to play. 'Have I told you lately how much I love you, Mrs Kennedy?' he murmured, his lips grazing her cheek. She smelled of baby powder and shampoo and he felt his body stir because it was a surprisingly potent combination when Sophie wore it.

'Not since seven o'clock this morning,' she replied as she wound her arms around his neck. 'Tut-tut, Dr Kennedy. A woman might start to think you didn't care for her after a lapse like that.'

'And she'd be right, too.' He kissed her lingeringly then reluctantly drew back because he knew from experience that when the twins were awake it was unwise to indulge in such delights.

'I don't care a jot for that woman but I care an awful lot about you, Sophie. I love you with all my heart. You and the twins have made me so happy that some days I think I'm going to burst.'

'Then maybe you won't be able to handle any more good news.' She looked at him consideringly and Liam frowned when he saw the excitement in her eyes.

'What's going on?' he demanded. 'What are you up to now?'

'It's not what I've been up to…well, it isn't *solely* my fault. You have to share at least half of the blame.'

She kissed him quickly then took his hand and placed it on her stomach. 'Guess what we're going to have in six months' time, Liam?'

'You don't mean… You can't be…'

'I am! Congratulations, darling. You are about to become a father—again!'

Modern Romance™
...seduction and
passion guaranteed

Tender Romance™
...love affairs that
last a lifetime

Medical Romance™
...medical drama
on the pulse

Historical Romance™
...rich, vivid and
passionate

Sensual Romance™
...sassy, sexy and
seductive

Blaze Romance™
...the temperature's
rising

27 new titles every month.

Live the emotion

MB3

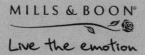

MILLS & BOON®

Live the emotion

Medical Romance™

THE BABY BONDING by *Caroline Anderson*

Surgeon Sam Gregory is the last person midwife Molly
Hammond expects to see. She once carried a child
for him and it led to a special and unspoken bond
between Molly and Sam. Now a single father, Sam
gives her the chance to get to know his son, but
Molly's bond with Jack leads to an even greater bond
with his father. If Molly enters into a relationship with
Sam now and it all goes wrong she may never see
either of them again...

IN-FLIGHT EMERGENCY by *Abigail Gordon*

Airport nurse Fabia Ferguson has kept her love for
handsome pilot Bryce Hollister close to her heart for
years. When he walks back into her life Bryce is
attracted to Fabia; it's an attraction he feels he can't
pursue because she reminds him of too many painful
memories – memories that made him give up his
medical career!

THE DOCTOR'S SECRET BABY by *Judy Campbell*

When Dr Lucy Cunningham hires a new doctor for
her practice in the Scottish Highlands she's not sure
about Callum Tate's laid-back lifestyle. But, forced to
live and work together, their passion quickly fires –
and then a baby is left on the doorstep, with a note
claiming that Callum is the father!

On sale 3rd October 2003

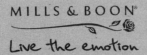

MILLS & BOON®

Live the emotion

Medical Romance™

THE ITALIAN DOCTOR'S PROPOSAL
by Kate Hardy

Lucy Williams was hoping to get the new consultant post at the maternity unit where she worked — but it went to drop-dead gorgeous, half-Italian Nic Alberici. Immediately sparks flew between them — until Lucy's former fiancé started pestering her and Nic came up with an outrageous proposal: that they pretended to be an item...

A CONSULTANT'S SPECIAL CARE by *Joanna Neil*

Dr Abby Curtis starts her new job in A&E with trepidation. Consultant Jordan Blakesley is notorious for his cutting criticism, and she's had enough of overbearing men! But he's so attractive that she cannot keep her eyes off him! And then dramatic events in Abby's life result in Jordan paying her very personal attention...

A CHILD TO CALL HIS OWN by *Sheila Danton*

Dr Ben Davey longed for a family, and meeting beautiful single mum Dr Tamsin Penrose was his dream come true. Until Ben discovers that Tamsin's child is the son of Ben's cousin — a man who disappeared mysteriously from his family's midst, several years ago. It unleashes a conflict and a tension that Tamsin believes makes a relationship with Ben clearly out of bounds...

On sale 3rd October 2003

Available at most branches of WHSmith, Tesco, Martins, Borders, Eason, Sainsbury's and all good paperback bookshops.

0903/03b

MILLS & BOON

The Pregnancy Surprise

Emma Darcy

Caroline Anderson

Gayle Wilson

When
passion
leads to
pregnancy!

On sale 3rd October 2003

*Available at most branches of WHSmith, Tesco, Martins, Borders,
Eason, Sainsbury's and all good paperback bookshops.*

FREE
4 BOOKS
AND A SURPRISE GIFT!

We would like to take this opportunity to thank you for reading this Mills & Boon® book by offering you the chance to take FOUR more specially selected titles from the Medical Romance™ series absolutely FREE! We're also making this offer to introduce you to the benefits of the Reader Service™—

- ★ FREE home delivery
- ★ FREE monthly Newsletter
- ★ FREE gifts and competitions
- ★ Exclusive Reader Service discount
- ★ Books available before they're in the shops

Accepting these FREE books and gift places you under no obligation to buy; you may cancel at any time, even after receiving your free shipment. Simply complete your details below and return the entire page to the address below. *You don't even need a stamp!*

YES! Please send me 4 free Medical Romance books and a surprise gift. I understand that unless you hear from me, I will receive 6 superb new titles every month for just £2.60 each, postage and packing free. I am under no obligation to purchase any books and may cancel my subscription at any time. The free books and gift will be mine to keep in any case.

M3ZED

Ms/Mrs/Miss/Mr ....Initials ....
BLOCK CAPITALS PLEASE

Surname ....

Address ....

....

....Postcode ....

Send this whole page to:
UK: FREEPOST CN81, Croydon, CR9 3WZ
EIRE: PO Box 4546, Kilcock, County Kildare (stamp required)